Mr. M's Notebook:

High School

A Teacher's Life

A Trilogy
By John Splaine

Mr. M's Notebook
Book Two: High School
Copyright © 2019 by John Splaine

This is a work of fiction. The characters depicted in this novel are not associated with any person living or deceased. Any resemblance is unintended and coincidental. The events, except those that can be verified as historically accurate, did not happen.

Published by Piscataqua Press
An imprint of RiverRun Bookstore
32 Daniel Street | Portsmouth NH | 03801
www.riverrunbookstore.com
www.piscataquapress.com

ISBN: 978-1-950381-14-2
Printed in the United States of America.

For Art and For Sarah—

Never forgotten.

Table of Contents

Chapter 1: "Potluck"

In our midst was THE Lydia Smith—the student who had settled next to her social studies teacher, Derek Randallston, in a parked car at the end of spring break in April 1975.

The Gorham, Massachusetts superintendent of schools, Mitchell Appletone, had commanded that I inform Derek, a teacher in Bailey T. S. Memorial High School, that he was fired and should leave the school immediately. As far as I could tell at the time, Derek's only transgression was that he sat in a parked car with a student. The superintendent of schools removed Derek Randallston from the faculty because of what appeared to be happening.

At a potluck dinner on a Friday night, I discovered that the student—alias Lydia Smith—who had been sitting in the car with a teacher when a policeman came over, was an elementary school teacher in the Gorham school system.

My name is Mark Blenchard. The students call me Mr. M. In the late 1960s, Bailey High students began calling their teachers Mr. or Ms. and the initial letter of the teacher's first name. The tradition has continued.

In 1970, I started teaching in the social studies and

history department at Bailey T. S. Memorial High School located in Gorham, Massachusetts. I assumed chair of the department three years later.

My wife, Ana, and I have hosted periodic dinners with teachers in various subjects and grade levels. We hold the sessions at our home to discuss personal and professional issues and have done so since 1973.

We thought that meeting occasionally with colleagues would benefit us all. The potluck group assembles when our schedules permit. Over the years, we have talked about personal, local, national, international, and school issues. We also discuss our daily work as educators.

Nancy Cash, Ana's colleague at Gorham Central Elementary School and a participant in our dinner group, took maternity leave for the 1986-1987 academic year. Her problematic pregnancy hampered her return to teaching. She also decided to forgo the Friday night potlucks.

In addition to needing rest, Nancy told Ana, "Another reason for bypassing the dinners is for my health and for my baby. I need to stay away from the temptation of wine, deserts, and my tendency to occasionally eat what I shouldn't eat."

I grasped the culinary temptation's rationale. I lacked the willpower or even the desire to stay away from the potluck's bountiful table, and, as I imbibed, I self-talked, "If it does not kill me, oh well,"—my flimsy way of giving in to my weakness to quantities of food, rich and otherwise. I further rationalized that if the comfort food comforts me, "Then, what is the harm?" Fooling myself had worked so far, but I realized my out-of-control appetite may eventually have consequences.

Nancy Cash was wise enough to avoid the urge to indulge and took leave from the school system and from our potluck dinners. With Nancy on leave, the school system employed April Danniels for the year to teach at Gorham Central. Ana immediately recognized and appreciated her new colleague's wit, knowledge, and worldliness. We invited April to take Nancy's place at our Friday night dinners while Nancy was on leave. April accepted.

Our first potluck of the new school year was on Friday, September 26, 1986. English teacher Cheryl Wattsen, art teacher Karla Betts, social studies teachers Charles Yates, John Browne, Claudia Pace, Zack Barber, Jake Spanner, and Megan Straffa attended. Ana and I hosted. Gorham Central Elementary School teacher April Danniels joined in for the dinner discussions as Ana's guest, replacing Nancy for the year.

We continued to find our occasional potluck dinners personally and professionally rewarding. We all looked forward to each session as we shared personal reports and ideas. None of us missed the chance to attend unless a personal matter, professional obligation, or an emergency summoned us elsewhere.

As our group assembled, I asked the group to introduce themselves to April.

"I am Megan Straffa. I teach social studies in Bailey High, and clash with Charles."

"I am Charles Yates. I teach social studies in Bailey High with Megan. I agree, Megan and I clash."

"I am Zack Barber and teach social studies in Bailey High. I get a kick out of it when Megan and Charles go at each other."

"Hi, I am Claudia Pace. I teach in Mark's social studies department in Bailey High, where he is the chair."

"I am Jake Spanner. I also teach with Mark in Bailey High."

"I am Karla Betts. I am the only art teacher in this group. I, too, teach in Bailey High."

"I am Cheryl Wattsen and teach English in Bailey High."

"Welcome April to our dinner and discussion. I am John Browne and I teach social studies in Bailey."

"April, you already know Ana and me. Ana knows you because you both teach in Gorham Center Elementary, but the rest of us do not know you or much about you, so would you please tell us something about yourself?"

"Thank you, Mark. And, thank you all for inviting me to join you. Are you sure you want to know about me?" April flashed her wit.

"Yes," I said with a laugh.

"Okay. How much do you want to know?"

"Whatever and as much as you want to tell us."

"Well, Mr. M., and everybody, the first thing I need to tell you is my birth name."

"Isn't your name April Danniels?"

"No, that is not my birth name."

"Hmmm. What is it then?" I asked.

"April Danniels is my name now. I have had it changed legally. Someday, I might change it back to what it was. I am not sure whether I will or not, but if I do, it probably won't be for a while."

"This is getting interesting," Megan said. "Why then would it matter what it was before?"

"I think it might to this group. You must not have recognized me because of my appearance, my hair color and shape, and other parts of the rest of me have changed a lot. Most of you have seen me before. Does Lydia Smith ring a bell?"

"Waaaaait a minute. We had a Lydia Smith as a student over a decade ago. You can't be that Lydia Smith, can you? You do not look anything like...although if I

10

work on it, I can see a resemblance."

"Yup, Mr. M., one and the same—the former Lydia Smith is now April Danniels. I am that Lydia—the student who was in the parked car with Mr. D. Yes, I was with Derek Randallston in April of 1975—over a decade ago. Even though it was a while ago, I can picture and still recall the incident as if it were yesterday."

"Wow! You look so different." Megan exclaimed. "I am having trouble remembering the younger Lydia Smith and what she, I mean you, looked like."

"Yah. I lost some baby fat, gained some muscle weight, straightened my teeth, and added an inch or two in height. I started and have continued an exercise regimen. Also, I changed my hairstyle and color. But I am still the same person, just older, and hopefully, wiser and more mature."

"Lydia, this is hard to believe. Oh, I mean April. Sorry," I said.

"Yes, please, I prefer April. At least for now, that is the name I am going by. It allows me to be incognito until I can safely reveal my past to others. I realize I just told you my 'secret,' but I hope I can feel secure with this group. I assume it is the case that I can feel safe talking with you about what has happened in my life."

"Yes, your story is safe with us," I said. "As far as we are concerned, it is your call when you decide, if ever, what you want to reveal to others."

"That might take some time, Mr. M. Maybe, but just maybe, I may change my name back to Lydia someday. I like Lydia, but I like the way I came upon the name 'April.'"

"Why, did you say 'safely?' And, how about the name change?"

"Well, Mark, or may I still call you Mr. M.? I think

11

that is a cool name."

"Sure, April, call me whatever you wish."

"Mr. M. it is."

"Fine with me, April."

"I think you all will see why I want to control my narrative when I tell my story and why being safe in telling it is important to me."

"I remember you disappeared after the 'happening,' so to speak, with Derek. We had no idea where you went. And, we have no idea where Derek has gone either. Where in the world did you go?" Cheryl queried. "As you may remember, I love stories, so I am waiting anxiously to hear your story."

"Yes, Ms. C., I remember you love stories. I had you in English and absorbed a lot in your class. Thank you. I enjoyed your class and learned to value and learn from literature in your classes. Since I left Gorham, reading literature about people has kept me out of trouble and sane, at least for the most part.

"In Bailey High, I really liked my social studies teacher, Mr. D. I felt awful when he was summarily dismissed. His firing continues to haunt me. I gained a lot of knowledge in the history class I had with him. When I heard that Mr. D. had been fired, I surmised that it was because a police officer found me in a car with my teacher. I had trouble living with myself. I decided not to return to school. I wanted to just drop out of sight. When the police informed my parents that I was found in a parked car with a teacher, they were royally 'pissed off.' Pardon my language, but my mother and father were not happy when cops knocked at the door and told them where a policeman found me and who he found me with. My parents left a message for me. When I returned home, it was clear I was in a mess. I definitely did not want to face them."

"Oh, by the way, April, don't worry about your language in this group. We have Megan. She uses swear words most of us cannot recognize and haven't heard before," Charles said, half in jest.

"You do understand this one though—screw you! Don't you, Charles?" Megan exclaimed.

Charles smiled. "Like I said...."

"April, as you can see," I said, "we pardon your language and we usually pardon each other except when it goes overboard. Now, if we could get back to your story."

"Okay, Mr. M., I can see that you all know each other pretty well. You seem to accept each other as people. I like that and hope you accept me for who I am—April Danniels—formerly Lydia Smith. So, I will continue the story of what happened to me during and after that spring break in 1975.

"After being in the car with Mr. D. and realizing that a policeman had made a record of my being in a car with a teacher in a dark area, I decided I might have to leave Gorham. In doing so I would leave my home and hometown behind for I didn't know how long. As you can see, though, not forever—but, I believe long enough. Time has allowed for some forgiveness on my part and I think my parents, even though there are incidences I can't forget. While away from Gorham, I think I put myself together, or as together as I can be. So, here I am—for good or ill."

"Bailey High staff made multiple attempts to reach you and your parents, but we had no luck. You were eighteen years old, so even though you stopped attending school and we did not hear from you or your parents we assumed that you dropped out of Bailey High. We suspected your parents did not want to talk about what had happened.

13

"Now you have shown up in town over a decade after you left Gorham, and you have returned as a teacher nonetheless—Holy Cow!" I said. "So, if you would, please go back to Cheryl's question: Where did you go? And, Lydia, I mean April, here is a question of my own—what happened when you were away, and how did you get back here?"

"Okay, but I prefer everyone just call me April. That is my name now. Changing my name has helped me push some of the nightmares into my subconscious. The memories are still there and come back to haunt me now and then—like what happened with Mr. D.—but the name change has helped somewhat. I forgot, Ms. C., what did you ask?"

"April, what happened from the time you left Gorham and how did you get back here? I can't wait to hear your account." Cheryl said.

"I would like to hear the story too," Megan added.

"Me too. I agree with Megan which doesn't happen very often, but it does happen now and then. It might even happen again when she says something that makes sense. So, April, what did happen next?" Charles asked.

"Oh, Charles...."

"Megan, PLEASE. You don't have to say what you are thinking. The rest of us want to hear what happened with April," Charles said.

"Ana knows some of it. Ana, should I tell it? It is a long story."

"Yes. April, it would be informative to all of us. The parts I know clarify some of your past and how your present status developed. However, I would like to have some gaps filled in. I can't wait to hear the rest of the story, or at least the parts you are able and want to tell us."

"I would like to have what I reveal to you be

14

confidential. I may write about it someday, but not yet. For now, anyway, I would like to keep it just within this group."

"As I indicated before, we are pretty good at keeping things close and within this group."

"I can vouch for Mr. M. on that. I have disclosed to this group things I would not want communicated to anyone else. This group is tight and considers what it hears privileged information—thank goodness." Claudia added.

"Well, here goes," April said. "When I heard about Derek Randallston's firing, I left school and contemplated leaving Gorham. I was sick to my stomach. I couldn't understand why he lost his job because nothing happened in the car. We were just talking about things. He was helping me work through some personal problems. Once I heard what happened to Mr. D., I did feel I had to get out of town, if for no other reason than to keep my sanity. When I got home, my parents were not there. They had heard about the incident and left a note making clear their outrage over my involvement. It was evident that I was in a shit-load of trouble—in the parlance of the day.

"I packed some clothes, found sixty dollars I had squirreled away in an old purse. I grabbed a bag of 'rainy day' change in my dresser and was as ready as I could be to leave town. I thought I had no choice but to run from trouble.

"I called a friend who agreed to drive me to the bus station in the next town. I begged her to hold off telling anyone where she left me off. Mr. M., Ana, and everyone, as I boarded the bus my travails were about to begin."

"I can just imagine. A young woman out in the world traveling on a bus without a place to go and heading to nowhere in particular without many resources....

Uggggg," Megan groaned.

"Yah, Megan, you have that right. I had not been getting along with my parents anyway. I was eighteen years old, so I just took off. I got on the bus heading for New York City. I hadn't planned to go to New York, but that was the bus's final stop so that is where happenstance led me.

"After the bus and a sandwich and soda at one of the stops, I possessed six dollars and some change when I got off the bus. I spent some of it on a breakfast sandwich and took as many condiments as I could stuff in my pockets, and off I went.

"It was April. The rising sun warmed the crisp air. The sun-lighted, darkening clouds heralded the coming of a spring shower. The spring weather gave me the feeling of a new beginning. I was in the big city. I was anonymous. I was alone."

Chapter 2: April

"Here I was in New York with no place to go and no one to go to. My first reality-check was that I needed a place to stay. I asked a by-stander where I should go. She said there were some hotels close-by. However, I did not have enough money for a hotel for one day never mind longer."

"So, April, what did you do?" Cheryl asked.

"Blurry-eyed after the long ride, I started marching uptown. I stepped up the street with no goal in mind on an avenue a whole lot more crowded than anything in Gorham. Once I fully realized I had no place to go and no money to go any place with—anxiety set in. Furthermore, the bus had traveled through the night, made several stops, so my sleep was intermittent at best. When I arrived in New York, it was around 8 a.m. Without much shut-eye, I had that dizzy feeling one gets when sleep-deprived."

"So, what did you do next?" Karla asked. "I hope this story has a good ending."

"Well, I saw this unassuming lady. I stopped and asked her, 'Is there a place I can go to rest? I do not have any money to pay for a hotel.' She responded, 'I think there is a youth hostel up a couple of blocks and around the corner. I recommend that you try that. I have heard they house college kids and youth your age. I don't know what it costs, but if you don't have much money, I don't think they will throw you out. They might let you stay for a day or two. Maybe if you help, you could stay longer. Good luck, young lady.' I proceeded up the street. As I got closer, I asked someone else where the hostel is. After meandering for a while, I found it."

"The suspense is getting to me. Then what?" Megan asked.

"April, you have to tolerate my nervous friend— Megan. Go ahead and tell your story at your own pace," Charles said.

"Calling me a friend is pushing it a bit don't you think—CHARLES?"

"Alright, I will move along, Megan and Charles. I can see you have a, let me say, unique relationship."

"You could say that."

"Yah. You could, Charles and I have collided over the years. But this is about you, not us, please go on April."

"Well, as you will see, my saga expanded. I figured I might as well give the hostel a try. I went in the front door of the hostel and looked around. I then encountered this older woman, a volunteer, maybe in her late fifties. She was quite helpful and very nice. I told her that I didn't have any money. She said there were some vacant beds and it would be okay to stay for a day or two. She asked me to register. I showed identification. She determined I was old enough at eighteen, so I completed a form. She supplied me with bedding and directed me to a room where I could settle for a while. I went to the available bathroom, washed my hands and face, and laid down. Four hours later I opened my eyes."

"April, I haven't heard these parts of your experiences. As Karla said, I hope there is some good news in this adventure. You have me on pins and needles. What did you do?" Ana asked.

"This is a great story. Keep going," Cheryl, the English teacher stated. "It has to have turned out alright. You are here."

"Yes, Ms. C., I am here. When I woke up in the hostel in New York, I had to recover from a deep sleep. After traveling all night, I was, to say the least, woozy."

"I can understand that—been there myself," said Megan. "I can't wait to hear your telling of the story. So, then what happened?"

"Megan and everyone, I soon realized I couldn't remain in the hostel forever. That is where Helen came in."

"Who was Helen?" I asked.

"Well, I could write a book about Helen. Without specifying her actual age, she told me she was in her middle to late twenties. However, Helen looked a lot older—and I mean a lot older. She swore she was giving up alcohol and drugs forever. I had the feeling that she had foresworn narcotics, etcetera, before. She seemed to have convinced herself that she would this time.

"Helen had taken upon herself the role of unofficial mayor of the hostel. She cleaned around the hostel, so they let her stay when she wanted to or sometimes when she needed a place to stay for more than just a while.

"Helen personified character. She was something else. I liked her and for some reason trusted her instantly. I am still not sure why, but I did. There was something genuine about this person who had clawed through her still young life and apparently hit bottom more than once.

"I asked her, 'Helen, how do people survive around this city when they have no money or job prospects and how have you survived if you don't mind me asking?'

19

I probably shouldn't have asked, but I did. I got more than I expected.

"Helen said, 'I don't know how others do it, but I do tricks.' As she said this, she pulled out a wad of money—a big wad of money and dangled it in front of me. 'I use this money to pay for hotel rooms when I am away from here or when I am not doing any jobs in the hostel to cover the cost of a room. I sometimes pay them here when I have money, like right now I have some. Other times I don't have no money because I spend it on shit, give it to bums, or get mugged by someone who don't know me. This hostel is good for me. When I am in another place, they want me to pay. I try to freeload, but it don't always work, and I pay. Otherwise I just fucking freeload. I like it here—seeing the college students and such. The college kids are smart. Occasionally, they talk to me and I learn something. Are you a college student?'

"I responded, 'No, Helen, I am not. Although, I hope to go to college someday.'"

"Helen said, 'That would be good, Honey. I never had a chance to go nowhere like that. My momma died when I was a kid, so I dropped out of school to make ends meet. My mother had worked in houses as a maid all her life. She also took care of people's gardens too. She had scabs all over her because of the sun. Momma never had sunglasses because they cost too much—my mother couldn't see me too good. After she died, I didn't have no place to live. She came over from somewhere in Europe. She didn't know much English—just enough so she could follow directions as to what to do at rich people's houses.'

"'Didn't you have relatives to take you in?' I asked.

"Helen said, 'Hell no. I had no relations except my mother. I never learned her language. I learned to speak from kids in the street. I know my English is not too good, but I get by. Maybe if I can go back to school sometime, I can learn how to speak more proper. Like you do, young lady, you speak right, and I don't. I am ashamed to speak sometimes because I ain't educated. I feel bad about that, but I must get money to eat and can't go back to school to learn things I never had a chance to learn.'

"I asked Helen, 'How about your father?' Helen answered, 'Oh, I never knew him at all. When I was old enough to understand, a friend of my mother told me that a man raped Momma. The friend said that he lived in a big house that my mother took care of. I was born after that rape. My mother died one day before my ninth birthday. She wanted to live until my birthday, but she didn't make it.'

"'Do you know who your father is?'

"Helen responded, 'Nope. And, I don't want to fuckin' know either, because if I did, I might hurt the bastard. Then they would throw my ass in jail for a long time. I been in jails, not for too long, but I been in there long enough to know I don't like them. Hey, honey, I don't want to talk about this shit no more. We need to get you some money. Honey, that is your name now isn't it?'

"Helen then said, 'Honey, you are kind of cute. You could do the same thing I done to survive—you look good enough to get top dollar. It is either that or you find yourself a sugar daddy. Or, maybe even another kind of job. I had one of those regular jobs in a shop once when I was sixteen years old, but I was no good at arriving on time, so they fired my butt. So, it's your choice, Baby—tricks, a daddy, a job, or starve.'

"I thought I knew but I figured I better make sure, so I asked Helen, 'What do you mean by tricks?'

"Helen responded, 'Oh my, baby, you don't know— my goodness—tricks is screwing, fucking, sucking, do I have to show you?'

"Sorry about the language, but I think you want me to be candid."

"We do, April, we do. So, what did you say to her 'show you' question?"

"Mr. M., I said, 'No, you don't have to show me. I am sure I understand your point now.' I then asked her, 'How long, Helen, have you been making your way in life this way?' Helen responded, 'Oh, I don't know. Ever since I was old enough. An older lady protected me from getting involved with traffickers. She died young like my mother. She had spots all over her, too.' I then said, 'Gee-sus, Helen, Gee-sus!'"

"April, if you were going to go along with this gambit, weren't you concerned about disease or anything like that?" Megan asked.

"Well Megan, and everyone, in high school—and this is one of those things I would like you to keep confidential—I had been sexually active. Maybe too active, so after Helen had defined 'tricks' for me, I then had a rough idea of what she meant by a 'sugar daddy.' By the way, it was my sexual activity and fear of disease and pregnancy that I was talking to Mr. D. about in his car on that April night in 1975. He was trying to help me. I should not have asked him to give me some advice because the time we were in the car got him in trouble, but my regrets now don't help him. I still feel shitty about it. Mr. D. told me at the time that I should ask a female teacher. He mentioned you, Ms. C."

"Oh, my. Me? Why did Derek Randallston recommend me? I don't know if I could have helped you. Besides, after one close call, I have since been reluctant to give advice about personal matters. But go on, April, it sounds like you have a good book in you that could come out of your travels and experiences. I would love to read your narrative including Helen's story. You could be an anonymous author, or you could use an alias, so you could tell everything. And, telling everything makes for best sellers," Cheryl said with a wink, "or, you could use your real name—Lydia Smith, or April Danniels or whatever—whatever works."

"Thanks for the suggestion, Ms. C. But, to go on. I didn't like the idea of becoming a hooker—you know, with venereal disease, and I could get roughed up or worse. So, I asked Helen how one could go about finding what Helen called 'a sugar daddy,' so maybe I would only be involved with one person—therefore, reducing the potential problems all the way from infections to jealous lovers.

"Helen advised, 'I'll tell you what honey. I will help you find some nice clothes. You go to a hotel where there is a businessman's convention going on. Pick out your possible targets, and then ask an older gentleman— the older the better, but not too old—you don't want no heart attack when he is pumping away—and ask him if he would like some company. You don't even necessarily have to do anything with him, just hang around with him and make him look good to his friends and such. You don't have to fuck with him much, and if he is old enough it might only be once or twice, and it won't last too long anyways. Just make sure he don't die while you are in the act—that could get messy—someone might call the police.

"'What do you think baby? And, hey, baby, what should I call you besides baby, or honey, or...? You might not want to tell nobody your real name, so they could track you down. And don't let no one take your picture either. Hey, baby, I got a name for you instead of honey or baby. How about April? It is a pretty name, and this is the month I met you.'

"I responded, 'I like that name, Helen. Thanks. April will be my name from now on. I have always loved the spring. In New England, spring usually comes in the month of April — sometimes in late April — but it eventually arrives. So, April it is. I need a change. April brings in a change of seasons and, hopefully, a change in my life.'"

"This story is publishable. I will edit it for you if you want me to."

"Thanks, Ms. C. If I ever write my tale, I will take you up on the offer. After I got a new name, I wanted to know about finding a daddy like the one Helen said I could find. I asked her again because I hadn't fully comprehended the task at hand. 'Helen, how do you go about finding sugar daddies? Is that what you do?' Helen responded, 'Hell, no. I ain't ever had a sugar daddy. I aren't as cute as you, so I do tricks and blow jobs. Guys love to get blown. That is how I get most of my dough. If I do a really good job, or the guy liked it a lot, I get tips. You, though, could probably make a bundle by finding a sugar daddy. You might never have to get in a prone position or do any of the stuff I do. Lots of guys just want company, especially the older guys or the guys who don't have wives no more. Oh yah, kid, do you do girls? I mean big girls.'"

"How did you respond to that?" Megan wanted to know.

"I said, 'Gosh, Helen, I hadn't thought about doing things with women.'"

"So, then, what did you say about doing women?" Megan followed.

"I didn't answer that last question. I thought about it later. I didn't tell Helen, but I must admit, Megan, I thought about it."

"So, April, what did you do next?" Karla asked.

"As soon as I could get ready, Helen and I went shopping. We agreed that if I spent her money, I would pay her back with five percent interest if I, in her lingo, 'landed me a daddy.' She said she was sure I would find someone. Besides, I needed the money to buy the clothes, so I told Helen that it was a deal, and that I would pay her back as soon as I could — even if I didn't hook up with someone. I really didn't think anything would come of this gambit, but it sounded plausible and I needed some fresh spring air."

"This story gets better all the time. Go with it, girl," Cheryl said.

"Helen and I took off up the street to the shopping district. We went into the first store we found where I could try on some clothes. Helen directed me to a rack that was to say the least risqué. I had remembered how Ms. C. dressed, so I moved over to the more conservative racks with some attractive pantsuits. Helen protested, but she eventually acknowledged reluctantly, 'Well, baby, you the one who has to wear this crap, so you choose. Remember, you got to pay me back, but I believe you should show as much skin as you can. You ain't looking for a job as no receptionist, so you might as well show what you got. But it is your life baby, so I guess you can wear what the fuck you want.'"

"I must say April, I am glad you remembered what I used to wear and that you thought enough of it to want to choose something like what I would put on. Besides, the more conservative look might have helped you land, as Helen would have it, 'a daddy,' rather than just a one-nighter. By the way, as you can see with what I have on tonight, I still dress conservatively and mostly with pant suits. When I teach, I sit on my desk a lot when engaging in dialogue with the students, so skirts might draw some attention," Cheryl explained with a sigh.

"Yes, Cheryl, as a student I was always impressed by how stylish you were when you came to teach at Bailey High. It intimidated me when I was in your class, but it made an impact. And, per Helen's suggestion, I was looking for someone more long term, so I figured the more conservative look would help me land a daddy," April said while laughing.

"But this gal, Helen, sounds like a real character; she was on your side. She has a book in her too, or a book about her," Ana offered.

"Ana, she sure was, and still must be a character," April agreed.

"Did you end up buying anything in the store?" I asked.

"Yes. I did. Two outfits."

"So, what did you get?" Cheryl eagerly asked.

"They were both pantsuits. Helen demanded that, if I was going to get pantsuits, one of them be fire-engine red. She said, 'You need to attract attention,' so she selected a red suit. Indeed, it sure would attract attention. I then chose a conservative gray for my choice. So, Helen and I each had our color—her red-red-red and my gray."

"Then what?" Ana asked.

"Well, Ana, Helen and I returned to the hostel. A big group had just come into the hostel to stay for a while. I really did not want to sleep in the hostel another night. Not because it wasn't fine for the time being, but I was anxious to get on with my life.

"I decided to find a hotel where there was a convention, so I could possibly find a man who needed an escort. It would be no more than just being with a guy who wanted companionship, or, at least, that is all I hoped it would be. I asked Helen where the ritzy hotels were, the ones that might be having conventions. She said there were several about ten city blocks away.

"Much to Helen's chagrin, I put on the gray suit instead of the red. I bagged the red suit and the rest of my worldly possessions and left my luggage in the room in the hostel. I was ready to hunt. I figured I might be back to stay and sleep in the hostel if I didn't find any other place to reside for a night or two. I then headed uptown. Helen wished me luck and waved goodbye with a whimsical smile on her face. I started up the street to find a man who wanted company, or as Helen would say, my 'sugar daddy.'"

"By the way, did you get a chance to repay Helen?" Jake asked.

"I tried. When I returned to the hostel to retrieve my worldly possessions, I asked for Helen's address to send a check to her when I had the money. However, the staff said she had already left and did not know whether she would be back. I got the mailing address of the hostel. Helen had registered so I obtained her last name. I sent a check when I had enough cash in my checking account. However, the check has never been cashed."

"Do you expect to ever see her again?" I asked.

"I would like to. If I do meet with her again, I would thank her, and hug her tight for as long as she would let me. I would cherish any moments with her she would let me have."

"I hope you can find her someday."

"Me too."

"April, I need to hear more about your adventures," Cheryl said. "There must be more—much more—because you did get back to Gorham."

"Yes, there is more. Okay, Ms. C., and everyone. Should I continue?"

"Please do. I can't wait to hear the rest of the story. I think I speak for the rest of the potluckers."

John Splaine

"Well, Ms. C., and everybody—here goes—the saga continues. After I changed my clothes into the gray pantsuit, I was ready to venture into the next part of my life. It was a beautiful spring day. The temperature hovered in the high sixties with a light balmy breeze, which, at that time of the year, New York found its denizens out and about.

"I sauntered up the street and spied a sign outside a hotel. The hotel looked big enough and rich enough to hold a convention populated by the kind of businessmen Helen advised me to look for. The sign indicated that not only was a convention being held but that there was more than one organization holding meetings. So far, so good.

"I went in the hotel through a revolving door. Now, I just had to score—so to speak."

"Hey, honey, what did you do next?" Karla asked with a coy grin. "I may need to find my own 'sugar daddy' someday. So, I need to know how to do it."

"Well," April said, "it wasn't as difficult as it may sound."

"Hmmmmm. Yah, sure, honey, but I don't look like you," Karla retorted.

"Right, Karla. In my pantsuit I looked very business-like—like a young college student looking for an internship. I did not look like I was hustling which may have been part of the attraction and the essence of the ruse. I went into the hotel that was hosting conventions and conferences. The hotel had more than one bar.

"I walked through the corridors looking for a potential hook-up. I peered into an open bar in the lobby area that had this guy seated on a stool alone. He stared at the mirror behind the bar, which displayed my reflection approaching him. It was the kind of upscale bar that looked like it would attract a well-heeled guy which was

28

the type, of course, that I was looking for.

"This guy was nursing a drink and looked like he might want company. I sat next to him. He looked at me like he wanted me to go away. I thought that I may have misjudged this guy's interest in having someone like me around—much less someone to talk with. So, I thought for a moment that I may have completely misread him. I didn't think I looked dangerous, so his evil-eye heightened my curiosity. As a cocky eighteen-year-old, I didn't think I looked that bad back then, so I wondered why this guy, maybe in his late thirties or early forties, was not interested in striking up a conversation with a young woman.

"I have never been bashful. So, I asked him the most obvious question I could think of, 'Are you here for a convention, a conference, or just hanging around?'"

"What the hell did he say to that?" Megan asked hastily.

"He said, 'I am here for a convention.'"

"Is that all he said?"

"Yup, Megan, that was it. And he said it with no expression in his voice or on his face whatsoever."

As I mused about what could have happened next, I asked, "Then what did you do?"

"Well, Mr. M., as you may recall when I was a student at Bailey High, I rebelled which got me into trouble now and then. I still don't like being quieted, and I thought this guy sitting at the bar may be expecting me to shut up and go away. After about fifteen seconds, I asked the next obvious question."

"Which was?" Cheryl asked.

"Sir, would you buy me a drink?"

"Well, what did this guy say to that?" Megan probed after a jibing laugh.

"He responded, 'Yes, sure, but first I would like to

29

know your name.'

"That seemed like a reasonable enough request. I responded, 'My name is April.'

"He asked, "Do you have a last name?'

"I said, 'Yes, but I don't give it out to just anyone.'

"To which he responded, 'Well, I guess I can understand that.'

"I said, 'Now that we are getting acquainted. What is YOUR name, or is it just Sir?'

"He said, 'My name is Carl Betcher. Or if you want to, you can call me what my friends do. They call me CB.'

"I said, 'It is nice to meet you Mr. CB.'

"'And, what should I call you?' he asked.

"I said, 'If you don't mind, I would just like to go by April.'

"He asked, 'Is that your real name?'

"I said, 'It is now.'

"'Interesting,' he said. 'How about if I call you Ms. April? It has that beauty queen sound.'

"'Please,' I said, 'just April is fine.'

"He said, 'April it is. Just call me CB.'

"I agreed and ordered a drink," April said. "After we started talking, it became clear that Carl Betcher was an easy guy to get to know and, as far as I could tell, he was trustworthy. I fessed up to CB. I told him that I was out of money, had run away, and was now homeless. I also told him that I was not a 'working girl,' but would do what was necessary to survive. I informed him that I was eighteen and legal.

"CB responded, 'April, you won't have to worry about me. I don't tell everyone this, but I am gay. So, you are safe with me. I vastly prefer men for physical intimacy. In fact, I am only intimate with men. You won't have to do anything at all. I prefer you not even touch me except for maybe a handshake or a high-five if we have something to celebrate. I have two double beds in my hotel room. If you want to, you can stay in my room tonight. I assure you I won't touch you, so please don't worry. I understand your situation. If you want to go get your belongings, you can stay in my room in this hotel. The room number is 1406. The room is already paid for, so it will not cost you anything.' He then gave me his extra key."

"Geesus, April, that was fast. Didn't you think he might be dangerous or up to something?" Megan inquired. "What did you do? And did you believe what he was telling you?"

"Well, I didn't have a whole lot of choice. And, yes, I did trust him. There was something about him that said 'safety' to me."

"You have more trust than I would have," Karla said.

"Then what happened?" I asked.

"I went back to the hostel, collected my clothes and personals, and looked for Helen to tell her that I may have found someone—at least to stay with. When I couldn't find her, I asked the receptionist where Helen was. That was when the receptionist said Helen had left and did not know where she went or when she would return.

"I then walked back to the hotel, found CB's hotel room, and moved my sole belongings in. I soon found out that CB meant what he said. He was a great guy."

"Was?" I asked.

"Yes. I said was. He died a couple of years ago. Had he not died, I may have stayed out West and never come back. At his remembrance service, I gave one of the eulogies. As a friend, I loved the guy." April paused as her voice broke. "Carl Betcher was kind to me. He never treated me other than with the full respect, I, as a human being and any other human being, should

31

expect and receive."

"So, you met this gay man, lived in his home, and ended up speaking at his service. What happened between meeting him in the bar and when he passed?" Karla asked.

"CB had money. He owned some businesses. He told me that he had inherited some money and invested well. After I returned to the hotel and put my luggage bag in the room, I went back to the bar. CB was still there nursing a drink. We started talking so I proceeded to fill him in on the rest of my story. I told him that I was in New York trying to get away for a while and maybe start a new life. After we talked about my situation, he said he was meeting someone but that in an hour I could come back to the room.

"I had no idea why I had to wait an hour. I spent some time in the lobby, had some free coffee and a couple of crackers, and went to the room after waiting for whatever I was waiting for. I had my bed for the night, and he had his. The next day, he asked if I would like to fly to Phoenix with him and stay at his ranch until I decided what I wanted to do. I told him that I did not have money for an airplane ticket. He said that was not a problem and that he would purchase one for me. At the time, I had no other home that I wanted to go to. I had never been to Arizona before and Phoenix sounded adventurous. I said, 'Sure. I am willing to go to Arizona with you.' We were on an early flight to Phoenix the next day."

"Well, you were eighteen then, and this is over ten years later. A lot must have happened over that time," Ana said.

"Yes, a lot did happen. It is a long story, but I will give you the essence of my journey from Gorham to the West and back.

"When we got to Phoenix, CB said I could have a room in his house. While living in CB's home, I worked jobs at coffee houses and restaurants. I saved enough money and took out loans to pay tuition and school expenses so I could attend a local university.

"CB said I could continue to stay at his place and commute if I wanted to go to school. I bought a used car cheap on credit with CB co-signing. I kept waitressing, completed my high school diploma, and enrolled part-time at the state university. I took nine to twelve credits a semester so, in effect, I was just about full-time. It took a little over five years to get my degree.

"In my first semester, I took a basic education course in which I had a great professor. This course hooked me on education. I gradually became determined to become a teacher. My professor believed in children's play and was highly experiential. She brought children into the classroom and we went out to area schools to observe and participate. We interacted with students in all grades. It was great. I decided I wanted to become a teacher—an elementary school teacher.

"I kept on working at various jobs and stayed in CB's home until he passed. Then the few relatives he had arrived and decided to sell the house. I moved nearer to campus, shared an apartment with some other students to keep my expenses down, kept working, and finished my degree.

"After graduation, I taught in Arizona for a couple of years and then in California until I decided to come back here—home if you will. When I saw the opportunity to teach first grade in Gorham on a temporary basis, I jumped on it. I applied and got the job. Even though it is only a year assignment, I figure if I do a good job the administration may find a permanent spot for me.

"Please though, as I said, I prefer the story I have

told you not get out to others in Gorham who don't know the full story. Telling part of the story could be misinterpreted. I still remember the fictional story Mr. M. told in class about going to a hotel for a meeting with his secretary and having a good time. If part of the story is left out or mischaracterized, then rumors start, and it's difficult to eradicate a rumor. Once a story gets started, it can be relayed with a totally different meaning than what happened—like in Mr. D.'s case.

"I would like to stay in this school system, teach, and help students learn. I was helped by my teachers here in town and want to give something back. I don't need any rumors floating around town about my past and what my life was like when I was away. In fact, the truth could be incriminating enough to some people, so distortions of my story would not be helpful," April said with a sardonic laugh.

"I hope they do find a permanent position for you, April. You are a great teacher and the children love you. And, I love you." Ana said.

"Thank you, Ana. I very much appreciate that. I feel the same about you."

"This is getting to be a little too warm and fuzzy for me," Charles said as he laughed with obvious irony.

"Charles, you know how to stop a good love-in," Megan said.

"We are about to call it a night. Anyone have anything else to say?" I asked.

"Do any of you have any more questions for me?" April asked.

"Like I said, April, you have a book to write," Cheryl said. "Your life has been interesting. I am sure there are more chapters yet to come."

"Hmmmm. I will think about writing a book, but first I have some students to teach," April said. "However,

Ms. C., I appreciate your confidence in me that I could and should write a book."

"I am certain of it. You have quite a story to tell—an important story."

"Speaking for myself," Ana said, "and I think the rest of us, we are glad to have you back in Gorham, Massachusetts, and as a teacher at Gorham Center Elementary."

"Thanks, Ana."

"By the way, have you seen your parents since you have been back here in Gorham?" I asked.

"No. They retired and are living in Florida. I plan to see them in November, for Thanksgiving."

"Did you see them or talk with your parents when you were away?" Karla asked.

"Yes, I did talk with my father and mother, but it has been sporadic. I talk with them occasionally on the phone—usually on birthdays and holidays. During my away period, I did not see them as much as I talked with them by phone. The last time I saw them was about three years ago. I met them in the airport in Dallas when they were on their way to San Antonio for a friend's funeral. It has taken a while for the anger to subside on both our sides—it has not gone yet. The Dallas meeting did not work out too well. So, this coming November during the Thanksgiving break will be my first time to be with them in person since Dallas."

"If you are interested, April, I believe I speak for the group in saying that we would love to talk with you more about your life and teaching as the fall progresses," I said. "I believe you might benefit from hearing about our lives and the issues we encounter in our teaching. How about coming to another potluck dinner and maybe more after that?"

"Mr. M., I would love to join you all as often as I

can. I feel comfortable with this group as people and as fellow educators. I want to be able to share things with colleagues and friends I trust," April expressed. "I am beginning to sense closeness with this group, and that I can call on any of you for assistance as I go on. I think I will need help as I get acclimated to teaching here in Gorham."

Chapter 3: Albert

Ana and I set Friday, November 14, 1986, for a potluck dinner with Albert Standwicke invited as a guest. After the tragic death of our student, Evan Gorges, school counselor Albert Standwicke and I asked each other variations of the questions, "What should we have done? What can we do for any of our students in the future?"

Evan died of a gunshot wound in the spring of 1986. Albert and I tried to understand what had happened. The stigma attached to suicide discourages and sometimes prevents us from even talking about it. We don't know what words to use to describe it — why it occurs, why there is so much of it, and what to do about it.

In our discussions, both Albert and I concluded that we must "dispatch shadows," and open our minds and hearts to young people who need our help and guidance. We agreed we must learn more—including what words we should use and what messages to convey. For the potluck dinner discussion on the fourteenth of November, social studies teachers Megan Straffa, Charles Yates, Jake Spanner, John Browne, Zack Barber, and Claudia Pace said they would attend. Karla Betts, an art teacher, Cheryl Wattsen, an English teacher, and April Danniels, who took the place of elementary school teacher, Nancy Cash, also could join us for dinner and discussion.

Albert said he hoped to join us for a dinner conversation. We invited him to be with us to exchange views about anything he wished. We generally gathered at 6:30 P.M. The number of participants at our Friday night potluck dinners has continued to grow since I began as chair of the social studies department in the fall of 1973.

In my earlier discussions with Albert Standwicke, he expressed his desire to meet with colleagues to try to make sense of the passing of Evan Gorges, a valued member of our school community. Albert wanted to know how he, in his role as a counselor, could better aid students who needed his assistance. We as teachers were also eager to know how we could help troubled students.

Albert grappled with multiple emotional issues while enduring some difficult weeks after the loss of Evan. When I passed him in the school's corridors, his face revealed his constant questioning over what he could have done to assist a student, and, in this case, conceivably save a life.

Seemingly without expecting or even seeking a response, Albert more than once asked me, "Mark, what could I have done to help Evan? What should I have done? Did I do all I could? Why did I fail a student this time? Have I also failed other students that I don't know about?"

Albert continued, "It is hard to live with myself when I fear I may have been unsuccessful at my most important job—aiding students as they are growing into adulthood. And, in Evan's case, he did not make it to adulthood. I blew it, Mark. I blew it."

As the dinner group gathered when Albert was

scheduled to join us, Ana asked, "Where is Albert? Mark, you said he was anxious to join us for dinner and participate in one of our potluck discussions. I thought you expected him to be here early. Are you sure he knows where we live?"

"Yes, Ana, he assured me he knows where we live. I believe he will be here soon. I confirmed the date the other day when I saw him in school. He told me, 'Mark, I can't wait.' So, I expect him to arrive soon. At least, I hope he will. If he wants to lead the discussion, I plan to have Albert open our conversation."

As more minutes passed, I said to Ana and the group, "Albert repeated our address and directions to our house. I gave him our phone number just in case. He may be on the road already. We are having one of those early winter squalls that occasionally swirl through Massachusetts in November, so that may be slowing him down.

"Anyway, there is no reason we can't begin our dialogue on a topic of the group's choosing until he joins us. Albert should be along shortly."

By now, we had dipped into our smorgasbord. As seven in the evening approached, I initiated the discussion even though Albert was not yet with us. I asked the potluck group, "Well, everyone, are there any personal, school, professional or political issues we need to discuss?"

The phone rang as I asked the question.

Ana answered, and then handed the phone to me. "Mark, it is for you," she said.

Albert, a lifelong bachelor, shared an apartment with his longtime friend, Nicholas Brooks. We didn't know much about Nicholas—just that he and Albert had been friends since college. I took the phone. Nicholas was on the other end.

"Mr. Blenchard, Albert asked me to call. He has had what appears to be a minor stroke. I took him to the hospital. They checked his vitals. As a precaution, Albert is staying in the hospital until he is well enough to leave. He was conscious and aware enough to ask me to call you and tell you that he is sorry about not making the potluck dinner tonight. As you know, he really wanted to join the group and engage in the discussion."

"I am so sorry to hear the news, Mr. Brooks," I said. "Is there anything we can do?'

"No, not at this point," he said. "And, please call me Nicholas. May I call you Mark?"

"Yes, of course, please do." I could not believe what I was hearing. I said, "I am so distressed to hear the news."

"I will call the school on Monday and inform the administration that Albert will not be in school until his physician says he is okay and able to return to work."

"Thank you, Nicholas, for letting me know about Albert. I must say, it is upsetting. May I tell the teachers here at dinner this evening about what happened?"

"Yes, Mark, please go ahead. Albert said he does not mind others knowing. In fact, he would want others to be notified what happened so rumors don't get started. Besides, Albert's absence will be noted around school by the end of the school day on Monday, so please do let his colleagues and friends know."

Educators care deeply about what happens to their students. Albert Standwicke certainly was one of those educators. Albert had attempted to support Evan as well as other students in the school. Those he assisted and comforted brought joy to Albert. Those he could not help deeply saddened and distressed him.

When events called for his help, Albert was instrumental in aiding Bailey High's faculty and students. The Space Shuttle Challenger exploded soon after taking off on January 28, 1986. A social studies teacher from neighboring New Hampshire traveled on the ill-fated mission. Albert consoled the school community as it grieved the space ship's disintegration and the death of its crew.

Seven American astronauts perished on board. Bailey T. S. Memorial High School's teachers and students mourned. With Albert's help, the faculty and students understood the risk the space travelers had accepted. From that January day in 1986, Albert centered himself inside the Bailey community.

After the news of what happened to Albert settled in, we decided to finish dinner and call it a night. The news about Albert shook our group. We agreed to try to schedule another potluck when Albert could be with us.

Albert rested a few days at home. He planned to return to school as soon as possible. Like most educators, Albert couldn't wait to get back to work with his colleagues and students—his life's work.

Once he recovered from the mild stroke and felt strong enough, Albert Standwicke returned to Bailey High. Soon thereafter, he registered for two courses in counseling at the local university. Conscientious to a fault, Albert intended to improve his skills. He told me, "I don't want what happened to Evan to ever happen to any other student I am responsible for and have the chance to help. I must know more, and how to explain what I learn."

At the rescheduled potluck for Albert to attend, he stood at our front door fifteen minutes early—too embarrassed to knock. Albert, ready and eager to come in, waited. We found him positioned on the bottom step dressed, as was his custom, in his blue blazer. As usual, he arrayed his signature red bow-tie on a starched white shirt.

"Albert, why are you standing out there?" Ana asked from the doorway. "We did not know you were outside waiting. Please do come in. Everyone will be here soon."

As others arrived, we congregated around the living room with our plates and drinks on trays. April Danniels had never met Albert, so I introduced them.

Ana knew Albert from discussions at school functions. "It is nice to see you again, Albert," she said. "I am so glad you could join us." The rest of the faculty of Bailey High had previously talked and worked with Albert at one time or another, so we dispensed with further introductions.

I called for everyone's attention. "As you know, Albert Standwicke is a counselor at Bailey High and is familiar professionally to most of us," I said to the group. "After Evan Gorges' death, Albert and I explored ways in which we can advise and strengthen students as they grow through the teen years.

"Now that Albert has recovered from his illness, he is able to join us. He just told me for his evening with us he preferred I lead the discussion and he be a participant. Therefore, I guess we can start with this question: What is it our students are going through that we need to understand and be aware of?"

"Mark, Albert, and everyone, I believe our students are under enormous pressure. In fact, I am sure of it," Megan asserted. "Our kids are under all kinds of stresses—academic, personal, appearance, social, physical, identity and so forth."

Ana added, "It could be bullying like Crissy experienced or the body-shaming our teens engage in or are on the receiving end of, sometimes from adults. Indeed, adults are much too frequently the 'shamers.'

"In addition, we should know better, but we constantly

pressure our children to do well in school and on the standardized tests, stressing that, as the argument goes, 'they will not be successful in life.' This is just too much for some of our kids. Also, I know that Mark's and my children, Joel and Suzie, are constantly pressured by this or that obligation. I try to get them to relax and go out to play but they say that they have no time to play outside and create. There is something wrong with this picture."

"Albert and the rest of you," I said. "what do you think?"

"Well, with two kids, Jennie and I have decided to homeschool our children, which should take some of the pressure off," Zack Barber said.

"How has that worked out, Zack?" Jake asked.

"Jake, it does take away some of the pressures of schooling. However, our children are still part of society. They watch television, participate in community activities, and have friends who attend private and public schools. So, there is no way to escape the stresses placed on children. It is almost as if being successful requires that a young person sacrifice their individuality. Preteens and teenagers in our society too frequently lose themselves in the process. In some extreme cases, it is at all costs.

"Furthermore, with the new technologies expanding, and with the multiple means of communicating that our youth have today, new stressors have become prevalent. Some use the new message-boards to humiliate others, even bully them through anonymous comments. Parents often don't have a clue.

"Body image affects a young person's self-image, including that of my children, but, hopefully, it does not define them. I want my children to decide who they want to be rather than defining themselves through images portrayed in the media.

"I wish Jennie were here for this discussion because we talk about this issue often. She will be sleeping when I get home, but because tomorrow morning is a Saturday, and I won't have to leave early for school, we will have breakfast together and be able to talk. I want to hear what she thinks about some of the issues we have brought up this evening, and will continue to bring up, because they are so important to the lives of young people. She sees the strains on our kids. Even though they don't go to a regular school, they still feel the stresses of all children, and Jennie and I feel them too."

"Television and movies communicate to young people what they should be like, and what they should look like. In many ways it homogenizes them," Cheryl Wattsen interjected. "According to the prevailing image-shapers, there is only one way to look, and there is only one way to act. The 'look' reshapes young people into the media's ideal people. After a while, they are no longer themselves. They adopt the televised public persona. No wonder so many young people don't know who they are. Media-imaging tells our students that they should not be who they are."

Karla Betts added, "Schools place young people in boxes. Too many schools, elementary through high school, emphasize standards and standardization. We delete differences in a society that claims to value individuality and personal responsibility, but we really don't allow kids to be who they really are. Helicopter parents don't let their children figure things out for themselves. The parents are control freaks. We try to put young people in the same sized square box, absent any deviation from the societally-manufactured norm."

Albert had something to say as the dinner group

was readying to disperse. "This discussion has been very helpful to me," he said. "I haven't had much to contribute to the discussion tonight because I want to listen to what the rest of you have to say. It is clear to me that you, as teachers, are aware of some of the problems we all must deal with. I may have taken Evan Gorges' death too much to heart."

"No Albert, we can never take the death of someone's child—which we all are—too much to heart," Ana insisted.

"I agree, Albert," Megan Straffa said, her voice breaking. "I don't think you have taken it too much to heart. We all felt Evan's tragic death. In fact, by taking it as hard as you did, you honor Evan and all the students we have the privilege to educate."

"I seldom agree with Megan," Charles Yates declared, "but I agree completely with what she just said, and, Albert, I have a lot of respect for you."

"Thank you for being my colleagues and having me here this evening. Friday nights are usually the night Nicholas and I do something. Because of the nature of his job, Nicholas generally only has Fridays for us to be together. Nicholas recommended that I join you for this discussion, and that I skip our night out. At his behest, I am here and glad I came. Nicholas works day and night as a tax accountant for several corporate clients. I hope I can come to dinner another time with you when the kinds of issues we have been discussing come up again."

"Of course, Albert. You are always welcome to join our dinner group. We wish you were a regular member of our potluck, but we realize that Friday is your night for being with Nicholas. Certainly, we will invite you when the issue of pressure on students comes up again. We need to understand more fully the pressures our society places on young people and its emotional, physical, and academic consequences." I said as we adjourned for the evening.

After "Sir" Ralph Giffin resigned as principal of Bailey T. S. Memorial High School in June of 1975, Rose Drouin succeeded him as our principal. Rose earned our trust immediately. Her unabashedly pro-student attitude spread swiftly through the faculty and staff.

Rose supported student aspirations; she advocated for them. When some in the community protested what they perceived as her willful "protecting" of students, she offered her resignation. Because the faculty supported her as our principal and the students respected her and appreciated the school atmosphere she helped create, the school board remained silent when she said she was ready to resign.

As Bailey High's principal for over a decade, Rose Drouin's leadership refreshed the school's community. Ralph Giffin had depressed staff morale. His blustering rants fumed without positive effect. Rose, on the other hand, invited and boosted faculty and parental participation.

High school students faced increasingly complex issues as the twenty-first century approached. With a principal who understood and valued students and faculty, Bailey T. S. Memorial High School developed as a safe place for teenagers.

With Principal Drouin's guidance and the welcoming educational environment, a nourished and increasingly healthful Albert Standwicke returned to his lifelong mission.

Chapter 4: "Lynching"

"You know, Mark, a person can be lynched in a variety of ways," John Browne stated in one of our increasingly frequent discussions.

"Huh, what do you mean, John?" I asked.

"We know what happened in this country after the Civil War. The Ku Klux Klan sought to make sure that the formerly enslaved people did not threaten white hegemony. Several states passed 'Jim Crow' laws and 'Black Codes' to make sure the former enslavers maintained control. Terror assured dominance.

"After the war ended, those released from enslavement paid a particularly cruel price, especially if they had cooperated in any way with the Union forces. Reconstruction did little to construct and improve life for the people recently freed. Reactionary forces betrayed the Thirteenth Amendment to the Constitution of the United States.

"The pre-Civil War system in slave-holding states did not change after 1865. Peonage followed slavery. African Americans tilled land for the plantation owners for a pittance. The white supremacist post-Civil War scheme enabled re-enslavement, albeit under a different name. This eventually led to the imprisoning of a disproportionate number of African Americans into the prison industry's pipeline. Some of the unshackled were jailed for vagrancy, some for loitering, some for other petty infractions, some for trumped up misdemeanors, some for talking back, some for fighting back, and some for being black.

"The violence against black people occurred mainly in the South but not exclusively. As I have said to you before, Mark, the North also had its ways to subjugate. Even the 'good people' in the north averted eyes from the injustices. Northerners assuaged their guilt and separated their conscience from what they said they believed and what they did. In northern states, segregated schools, segregated neighborhoods, segregated country clubs, segregated swimming pools, and anything else that could be was segregated. Some of the segregation was de facto, some because we knew we were not welcome, and some was illegal. The implicit and explicit separation of the races intended to protect white privilege.

"Physical lynching in the South occurred. Some of my ancestors fought back. They fought for themselves, their families, and the dignity of our race.

"Furthermore, Mark, those in power tried to lynch our personal dignity from us. My ancestors were willing to die to preserve our humanity. As you can see, this pisses me off."

"John. I get the anger and I understand most of what you are trying to tell me, especially the history," I said, "but lynching your personal dignity—I don't get that. What do you mean?"

"Well, I mean—our personhood was stripped from us—our human dignity," John explained with fervor. "It was as if our blackness could brush off if we rubbed up against white people. For some white people, the mixing of color was the worst thing that could happen. So, we were taken away—lynched—through segregated this and segregated that. We were rendered invisible, and still are to some people—maybe even to most people. If we stay away, then we are considered 'OK.' To the white power structure, we are tolerated only if we remain in our place. For some of us, my brothers and sisters, it has meant incarcerating us. And through recidivism, the prison industrial complex has fabricated an excuse to throw away the key and keep us revolving through the door."

"John," I said, "your characterization sounds too extreme."

"Sorry about that," John said, "but I define 'lynching as something done without the authority of law.' For example, no one says we won't educate black people or Latinos because to say so would be imprudent. However, our society does under-educate black people and other people of color, and we do it 'without the authority of law.' Our educational system just does it. You can call my assertion extreme if you want, but I believe it is reality.

"Our country under-educates, and in some cases miseducates black people. The lack of education leads to economic segregation, which leads to housing segregation, which leads to a whole host of other segregations. All purported and justified by the rule of law, but without the authority of law. As a result, a disproportionate number of economically segregated people end up in jail. I realize this is complicated, so let me explain further because there is a direct correlation between under-education and incarceration in the imprisoning system.

"After the adoption of the Fourteenth Amendment to the Constitution of the United States, with its provision for the '...equal protection of the laws...' we were supposed to educate all people equally—but we don't. We don't even come close. So, in that sense, those in power are lynching—taking away—without the authority of law—our human rights, and with that a chance to earn our own living. According to the Brown decision of 1954, it is not supposed to be happening, but in some cases the segregation today is worse than it was—say, in the mid-1950s."

"How do you mean it is worse?" I asked.

John went on, "We obfuscate the fact that education, for example, is unequal. We claim it is equal, but it isn't. Some folks get more education than others. It is designed that way, not necessarily on purpose, but due to the way the system works, that is the result. The elite and their children receive an exclusive education designed for them."

"What would be an example of that?" I asked.

"The numbers tell the story," John explained, sipping from his coffee. "By large margins, more white children are in the so-called 'gifted and talented' programs in elementary schools, and Advanced Placement courses in high schools. On the other hand, the 'commoners' receive less of an education—bigger classes, less-experienced teachers, and so forth. It just happens! Then we blame the victims who suffer the indignities and the inequities for not doing as well as the more privileged students.

"The chance for an equitable education affects our ability to make a living. Without an education—which I am arguing has for the most part been denied people of color—we are unable to attain good paying jobs, live in diverse neighborhoods, and live lives with our human dignity whole. Too frequently, a lot of us who are poor and lack an adequate education end up in the penal system and never get out. Our identities are lost—our persons vacated."

I nodded. "John, if you are right in what you are saying, we have some work to do. Do you have other examples?"

"Yes, I do, lots of them. Political gerrymandering is another instance of taking our civil rights and our human dignity away," John said. "Because of the creation of legislative districts that favor those in power, legislative protection and influence are taken away from minorities—our votes diminished.

"No law in the Constitution of the United States says you can gerrymander, although the Constitution allows ways for it to happen. The terminology derives from Elbridge Gerry in 1812, governor of Massachusetts at the time, who enabled the redistricting of congressional boundaries so one party would get more representation for fewer votes. The other districts were packed with stratified voters, so they would have fewer legislators representing their interests in the United States House of Representatives. Although legal, gerrymandering takes the ballot box away from selected people.

"In addition, there are a variety of ways in which voting is suppressed. The suppressor says, 'Sorry voter, there is a comma missing in your identification card. You can't vote, and it would be illegal for you to do so.'

"Therefore, Mark, you could add to the definition of lynch—political power that is unfairly taken away. Which, by the way, has profound implications for how people are governed. If we are underrepresented in government bodies, then we have less power to influence legislation. We are, therefore, ruled by others—others who might not have our best interests in mind. In fact, I don't believe a lot of legislators prioritize our best interests. The legislators do what their contributors and supporters decree they should do. We are not represented through this process.

"I realize I might be pushing the definition a bit, but I think you see what I mean. They are lynching our personhood—taking away our political representation and giving it to others. Do you get the point? You get it, don't you?"

"Yes, John, I believe I do," I said. "In fact, I am afraid I do. I don't like it, I mean, the truth of what I am hearing, but I believe I understand it."

"Mark, you as a white guy could say what I am saying. Why do black people have to be the ones speaking up about injustices? Why not white people, Mark? Why not you?" John asked. "Why don't you advocate for minority groups? Why don't you call the theft of our rights what it is—lynching. You could say that, Mark. If you, as a white man said it, it would get people's attention and have more impact. It would take some courage, but why not gut it out for fairness and for the good of the nation?"

"I believe that if I teach well, then that will help," I explained. "I am not sure what more I can do."

"Yes, Mark, teaching well is a start—but just a start."

"What then do you recommend we do about what you call 'lynching' of rights? Of political power?"

"Well, first, as you said, we need to teach about it in our schools. In some places, like Gorham, teaching about what is really happening in our country threatens the political power of the kleptocracy—so, that would at least be a start."

"Kleptocracy? What is that?" I asked.

As I asked John what a kleptocracy was, the bell rang. We were off to our respective classes. I planned to investigate the terminology—kleptocracy. When I did, I discovered it meant, "A government in which the rulers steal from their subjects." John had given me something else to think about.

Shortly after my discussion with John Browne, John traveled to Mississippi attempting to trace his family's genealogy. There he unearthed more than he expected.

John's great grandfather, twenty-four years old at the time, ran into a group drinking moonshine in rural Mississippi in the 1930s. John's great grandfather saw over twenty white men beating on a black man and asked them why they were doing it. The white men stopped what they were doing and said, "It is because he is a Negro." As John told me the story, he said the word used was not "Negro."

John's predecessor asked the mob if they would "please stop beating the man." When the perpetrators heard the request, they stopped beating the man long enough to turn to John's great grandfather. They beat him to death, filled his body with bullet holes, and then hung him naked upside down. John welled up and could not tell the rest of the story. He did have a contemporary picture recovered from a scrapbook kept by one of the participants who murdered his ancestor. I looked at the photograph—my entire being jerked.

"John, I can't look at this any longer." I closed my eyes.

As he saw and heard my reaction to the picture of his mutilated grandfather, John's eyes watered. He said, "Mark, I have to look, and I have to keep looking. He's my blood."

John's words stung me. I mustered the courage to look again—this time for a long time. I could not imagine what physical lynching was like. But as John has said to me, "The physical part may be a thing of the past—and I emphasize may be—but lynching is now accomplished in a different form."

"John, through our discussions over the years, I

realize in teaching here in Gorham's Bailey High I have barely scratched the surface of the predominate racism that pervades our town, school, and country," I said. "It isn't just in southern states, is it?"

"No, Mark, it isn't. Racism's ugliness is everywhere. It is shrouded here in Gorham," he explained tearfully. "If you look, though, you can see it. If you can still feel in this world of ours, then the extant bigotry is palpable.

"Mark, we can at least teach the historical record— that is the least we can do. Our students need to know that from 1870 to 1970, mobs murdered over 4,000 black men, women, and children. The attackers also killed more than 1,300 white people for daring to nudge the racial divide.

"In the period 1880 to 1930 alone, over 130 black women were lynched for 'disobeying their masters,' whatever that meant. I think, Mark, we can figure that one out.

"We will never really know how many people were executed, so I am probably supplying a conservative figure—those in power controlled the documentation. Those in control eradicated anything threatening white hegemony.

"However, the available records for the murders supply an idea of the horror. It takes nerve to teach about the terror, past and present. Some powerful people do not want us talking about the 'unpleasantness.' But think and teach we must.

"Furthermore, we need to teach the truth about our founders. Ten of our first twelve presidents enslaved people. Thomas Jefferson, the primary author of the Declaration of Independence, owned over 500 human beings. George Washington, our first president, ruled over 300. Presidents James Madison, Andrew Jackson, and Zachary Taylor each exercised dominion over 100 individuals."

John Browne wasn't finished unmasking the killing. "And, Mark, if the lynching mobs could not locate the man or teen they were looking for," he said, "the vigilantes lynched wives, children, or any family members they could find."

Chapter 5: "White"

Marsha and Richard Scranton invited Ana and me to dinner at their home. They had recently moved in next to us, so we gladly accepted the invitation. We wanted to get to know the people living on our street adjacent to us.

Ana and I should have invited the Scrantons first. However, prior to their invitation to us, our flimsy excuse to each other was that "we had not gotten around to doing so." Ana and I were looking forward to getting acquainted with Marsha and Richard.

Joel and Suzie were getting older and handled responsibility well, so we believed we could safely leave our children home alone. We cautioned Joel about being nice to his sister, and asked him to watch out for her. We didn't need to caution him.

Joel cherished his younger sibling. In turn, Suzie adored her brother. She had shadowed him as soon as she was old enough to crawl. Suzie always hoped Joel would pick her up for a hug and a swing or two. As they grew together, they occasionally engaged in brother and sister tiffs. Invariably, the siblings settled their squabbles before they went too far.

Suzie loved being with her brother, but insisted that

she could take care of herself. In case we needed to get home quickly, the Scrantons' home was within easy walking distance.

While serving drinks, I asked, "Marsha and Richard, where have you lived prior to moving to Gorham?"

"Well, Mark, we have lived all over," Marsha said. "My job has taken me to all sections of the country and some other places around the world."

"What kind of work do you do?" Ana asked.

"I am in information systems security," Marsha explained. "It is a relatively new field and much in demand."

"You mentioned you lived in many places," Ana said. "Where over the years?"

"Ana, you and Mark have many questions," Marsha said playfully. "It will be our turn next."

"Sure, Marsha. We value getting to know our neighbors and will be glad to share with you," Ana agreed.

"Ana, you asked where we had lived before Gorham. After we got married, we lived in California. Then we resided in communities in the midwest, the southeast, and now in New England.

"We usually stayed in one place less than four or five years. As you can see, we move around a lot. We are getting to the age where staying in one place appeals to us. Furthermore, our children want to stay in the same school for a while, so we hope to stay in Gorham at least until our kids graduate from high school. In addition, the college choices in Massachusetts are good ones. As residents of the state, tuition costs are another reason to stay here maybe even until retirement age," Marsha said.

"Richard, we have heard from Marsha about her work. What kind of work do you do or have done?" Ana asked.

"Ana and Mark," Richard said, "you do ask a lot of questions."

"Yes, we do. It's the educators in us," Ana said.

"I was a computer programmer for the first four years out of college," Richard explained. "Since then, I have mostly worked as a contractor—primarily with government agencies. As Marsha has had new opportunities, I have been able to follow her because I work independently. All in all, I am a well-kept man." Richard laughed.

"Yes, Richard has been good about re-locating with me as my work prospects have required us to move," Marsha said. "I very much appreciate his willingness to do so. It is usually the woman who follows the man."

"How far do you have to commute, Marsha?" I asked.

"Most days, depending on traffic, about forty-five minutes. Around here, commuting is measured in minutes, so I am not sure how far it is," she said. "I will have to check the mileage so the next time I am asked I will know. My office is just off the Route 495 beltway.

"How about you two, Ana and Mark? We have been answering all the questions and doing the talking. What has life been like for the two of you?" Marsha asked.

"I have been teaching here in Gorham since 1970," I explained. "I love my job, my colleagues, and the students I have had the privilege to teach here in Bailey T. S. Memorial High School.

"As long as administrators and some community members do not interfere with my work with students, then teaching here in town is what I have done and want to continue to do. There are some local politics in the Gorham school system, but if you know what they are then teachers can usually meander around the verboten strictures and teach with minimal interference.

"In Gorham, Marsha and Richard—as you will soon find out if you haven't already—teachers do have to watch out for saying or doing anything that is too controversial. If you do say something out of the accepted norm, the guardians will come down on you. The canon of what can be taught is pretty narrow in Gorham unless you know where the political parameters are."

"That is interesting," Marsha said, leaning in. "Please give us details about the politics of teaching. And, specifically, what are the politics here in Gorham?"

"Well, as I mentioned, you will discover Gorham is a conservative place. Much more so than in some other Massachusetts communities," I said. "The politics of a place, whether liberal or conservative, don't usually cause a problem if you know what they are and stay away from certain issues. Teachers need to know what the social and political environments are like in which we work. In Gorham, anything out of the conventional is challenged. A teacher in this community has to be aware of where the red line is, and what might happen if that line is crossed."

"That makes sense. I have run into politics in every job I have had," Marsha agreed. "There are political considerations in any profession."

"Yes, I agree Marsha. However, my job in teaching history and social studies is to present knowledge and get students to think. Some in the community do not want their children thinking and making up their own minds," I said. "A teacher needs to be aware of the community's political leanings and teach around them. Occasionally, a teacher has to have the gumption to bend or even push through a community's biases."

"Hmm, Mark, I need to think about that," Marsha said. "I hope we learn more over time about politics in Gorham. How about you, Ana? I hear you too are a teacher. Is that right?"

"Yes I am. I find the conversation so far very interesting. Except during occasional Friday night dinners with colleagues, Mark and I don't talk about our work at home," she said. "So, it is informative hearing from my husband about his work. So, Mark, I am listening."

"Yes, honey, I realize we don't talk much about our work at home. My ears are open to hear what you have to say, too," I said with a smile.

"Mark and I learn about each other when we are with other people explaining what we do," Ana continued. "Generally, Mark and I don't say much about our work when we are alone together. Our together time is precious to both of us and is usually focused on family.

"Well, with that said, here is my story. Joel and Suzie entered our lives early in our marriage. I went to work when Suzie was old enough to attend pre-kindergarten. I have been teaching ever since. I love teaching here at Gorham Center Elementary School as much as Mark enjoys Bailey High.

"I work with some great educators. Some have become close friends, especially Nancy Cash who is on leave this year but has been teaching at the school for as long as I have. I am also close to April Danniels who is relatively new to the school. Teaching at Gorham Center has been rewarding for me and I hope for my students."

"So, Marsha and Richard, now that we have answered some of your questions, here is another one for you," Ana said. "Why did you choose to move to Gorham? There are other possible places to live in the area and some must be closer to your work. So, why here?"

"That question is relatively easy for us to answer," Marsha said, sipping her drink. "Our major motive for moving here is because, Mark and Ana, we have found schools to be 'white' here."

"I am sorry. I am not sure I understand," I said. I took a sip of my own drink. "What do you mean by 'white' school?"

"Well, when we lived in the mid-Atlantic region, we chose to send our kids to a private school because there were few minorities in the school," Marsha explained calmly. "We try to send our children to schools that are populated primarily by white students—a few minorities here and there are okay—but very few.

"We aren't prejudiced or anything. We just prefer to be with white people who are more like us—have our values—and so forth. We have nothing against the others. We just want to live away from them and do not want our children going to school with them. And, Ana, we realize you are biracial, but you act whiter than others like you. Besides, you are a teacher and seem to be more like us than not—so we are okay with you living so close to us. All in all, you see, we do not have a problem living here in Gorham and sending our children to mostly white schools and having you as neighbors."

After those comments, we quickly changed the subject to the variable weather in Massachusetts where the climate is as unpredictable as what we just heard. We had no idea our new neighbors would say they now live in Gorham so their children can go to school primarily with white people, and that Ana was okay because she was not like the "others." Most bigotry we ran into was covert. We had seldom heard it spoken so overtly.

Ana and I returned home after dessert. We scooted Joel and Suzie away from card playing and the television set, and sent them to their bedrooms. After our children went upstairs, Ana and I discussed our curtailed dinner discussion with the Scrantons.

We talked late into the night about what we had

heard. "White" schools are essential for the Scrantons to live in Gorham, and we are "okay" as neighbors. We didn't respond at dinner. What we heard had left us speechless.

Ana and I finished our conversation that evening with a stream of questions: At dinner this evening, after hearing the Scrantons' rationale for moving to Gorham—so their children can go to a "white school"—what should we have done or said? What would John Browne have said or done? Why should John be the one to speak up and act? Why not us? If we don't speak up now, when will we?

Chapter 6: Julia

"Mr. M., why can't we read the book in Ms. J.'s class?" Rita, a sophomore at Bailey High, asked me.

Julia Brack, a new English teacher at Bailey High, had assigned a book for her students to read. The book featured a high school student's memoir recounting a gay student who endured repercussions after announcing he was "coming out" of the "dark place" he believed society had put him in.

I asked Cheryl, the chair of the English department, "Do you think using the book will continue to be problematic in this community?"

"Mark, yes I do. Because of Ms. J. using the book in class, some Gorham parents are vigorously protesting their children reading it. The critics are stepping up their attempts to censor the book. According to the critics, 'the book is smut and no one should be reading it.' I am not sure what to do or what will happen."

In the latter part of the twentieth century, it was beginning to be possible to walk out of the closet into societal sunshine. But in Gorham, some parents and citizens wished that those who were lesbian, gay, bisexual, transgender, or queer would stay quiet about it.

A comment frequently heard: "If they are going to make noise about who they are then they should get out of OUR town and its environs. Get out of Gorham and take your immorality with you. We, the good citizens of Gorham are telling you—if you are homosexual or not a straight heterosexual, go as far away as possible from Gorham. We don't want you here."

Cheryl further reported, "In response to complaints and challenges to the book, and without a public hearing, Gorham's school board has decided in executive session that 'until further notice the book cannot be assigned for a class, and it will henceforth be banned in the school media center.' The school board added, 'the book should never have been assigned in the first place without board approval, and the teacher who encouraged its reading should be disciplined.'"

After hearing that the book had been banned for use in all classes, and no copies would be available in the media center, Rita, who was in class with Ms. J. for English and me for history, asked me again, "Mr. M., why can't we read the book and why is Ms. J. in trouble?" I did not have answers to my student's questions.

The parents who protested Ms. J. using the book "demanded the school board pull the book out of the classroom, and any mention of it forbidden in the school."

As far as the critics were concerned, "the book is an example of moral degeneration and anyone who would write such a book must be a degenerate. Therefore, this trash must be banned in Gorham's schools."

The complainants also wanted Ms. J., a non-tenured teacher who was in her first-year teaching, "disciplined and/or fired because she had assigned the book which was not on the school's approved list. Her action in using the book in class is insubordination—a firing offense."

The petitioners argued, "If the teacher did not know,

then she should have known what she did was wrong. As a result of breaking the rules, especially one so important, she needs to be removed from Bailey High School classrooms immediately."

As a first-year teacher, Ms. J. was unaware of the school policy that only books that had been approved by the school board could be assigned to an entire class, which is what Ms. J. did. Maybe she should have known, but in teacher orientation sessions administrivia dominated the instruction for new teachers. Little discussion occurred about substantive matters—like censorship and the dangers Gorham's town censors could pose. Teacher orientation sessions often overlooked what was thought of as obvious, which was not so obvious to beginning teachers.

Julia Brack grew up in a wealthy suburb outside of Philadelphia, Pennsylvania. Her father worked as an administrator at a university and her mother as a practicing attorney. Julia's parents advocated and encouraged Julia and her brother to explore and pursue whatever it was they longed to do. Her brother enlisted in the United States Army. Julia chose to become a teacher.

As her parents did with her, Julia believed her students should make up their own minds about who they were, what they wanted to be, and what they wanted to study.

Ms. J., convinced that her students needed to read widely and deeply, wanted to assign books that provoked thought. Challenging texts, Julia Brack believed, would lead to discussing significant literature in her English classes.

The goal for her students was to transfer what they learned in the classroom to the world outside of school and then act on their beliefs. This was a radical concept for some Gorham parents and townspeople who wanted their children and students to replicate the world as their elders knew it.

After a week of relative quiet about the assigned book, the issue intensified when a student of Julia's, Earl, came out of the closet. That is when the trouble spilled into the public at large.

The censors reckoned, "because Earl had read the book in Ms. J's class, he 'turned' gay. Therefore, the teacher should be placed on leave until her fitness for teaching is determined."

Chapter 7: "Censors"

According to several of the critics, "Earl had made the choice to be gay. It is a clear case of cause and effect." The detractors believed that "reading the book encouraged and enabled Earl to reveal his homosexuality," and "he would not have done so if he had not read the book Ms. J. had assigned." They further contended, "the act of reading such a book might influence others; therefore, the 'trash' needs to be eradicated from the school and any mention of it in the school forbidden."

The critics stipulated that by assigning the book, "Julia Brack, the teacher, has excused homosexual activity by making it permissible to talk about it." Thus, sanctioning it for others to be "that way."

The act of "coming out" was something most of Gorham's citizens did not want to hear about—much less witness. Consequently, they claimed, "by having her students read the book, Ms. J. triggered all this trouble and 'gayness.' At the very least, she should be severely reprimanded."

The new superintendent, Dr. Clare McNeille, had taken over as superintendent after Mitchell Appletone's interim replacement, Denton Broon, "semi-retired" and went on to be a consultant in the state department of education.

Claire McNeille had earned a doctorate in education. Unlike Mitchell Appletone, she understood child development from kindergarten through high school. Dr. C. had also taught in various public schools for fourteen years which earned her credibility among teachers. Gorham's educators invariably declared that Clare McNeille was a "teacher's teacher."

Dr. C. favored an educational environment that accepted individuals, faculty, and students for who they were, and who they might become. She was ready and willing to support a student—any student.

Gorham's previous superintendent, Mitchell Appletone, managed through fear—dividing and conquering. Superintendent Clare McNeille built a climate of trust and cooperation.

Whereas Mitchell had tried to keep problems quiescent and out of the public eye, Dr. C. sensed that the community needed to understand why decisions were made. In a faculty meeting I attended, the superintendent said, "If people know why we do things then they are more likely to support what we do."

Dr. C. realized that the issue of the gay-themed book eventually required public involvement and—conceivably—civic approval. She recognized the community's need to know through a full hearing with stake-holders involved.

With Dr. C's encouragement, the nine school board members decided to hold a public hearing.

The school board held meetings on Monday evenings. The board customarily reserved time for its citizens to speak—allotting enough time for four speakers to speak for two minutes each prior to the board taking any action.

Ana and I hastily assembled our Friday night potluck group. I asked the group, "What should we do? What should I say? Or should we let someone who is not a teacher, but would represent our views, speak? If one of us does not speak, it might keep us out of trouble but then it might not. So, maybe we should just go ahead and say what we believe."

Charles commented, "It seems to me that whoever speaks is on his or her own. This is high stakes. You can lose your job for what the board perceives as supporting and condoning an insubordinate act."

"Yah, Charles, we can all lose our jobs if we support anyone who speaks against what becomes the board's decision. I just don't know what to do," Claudia said with a tenuous laugh. "Our union is not yet strong enough to defend us. And, as you know, I know something about losing a teaching job. Is all this worth it?"

"But Charles and Claudia, a discussion this important requires us to participate. We need time to present our case," I argued. "However, the board members clearly want to dispose of anything this contentious in as short a time as possible. Moreover, some board members most likely have already made up their minds.

"It will be first come, first-served to speak at the board's public hearing. I will sign up to reserve a spot for teacher input. If no one else wants to speak, I will do it. I have been at the school for a long time, and I am the chair of the social studies department at Bailey High. Julia is in the English department so as a member of another department I am somewhat detached, and the board may see me that way."

"Mark, maybe they will and maybe they won't," Charles interjected.

"Charles, I get the message," I said. "After signing up, I can withdraw before the meeting and let another advocate speak. I realize no one elected me, but in order to get at least one teacher heard I will act fast to place my name on the list. If another teacher wants to replace me and speak for Julia and the use of the book, then that is fine with me."

Before I had had a chance to sign up, a student asked to speak. Two community members had also registered to speak before I did and before the student. So, the community members were first and second, the student to follow, and I would be last.

"I understand what you are doing and why you are doing it," Claudia said, "but as I said, I know what it is like losing a job. I don't want that to happen to you, Mark, a guy I have learned to love and respect."

As I chuckled nervously at Claudia's comment, I said, "Over the weekend, I will think about what I might do. I can meet before school on Monday. Can you all meet with me, so we can talk further?"

"I can meet, Mark," Charles agreed, "but I hope you think hard and long over the weekend about what you might be giving up."

"Charles, I appreciate your concern," I said with a nod. "I will talk with Ana this weekend."

Everyone agreed to meet in the cafeteria over coffee before school on Monday, the day of the board meeting.

Ana and I needed to talk. I could still decline to speak. I realized I had to be candid with my wife about the downside of speaking out. I said to Ana, "If I get fired now, I could potentially lose my pension, and I am not yet near social security's retirement age. So, if I lose my job I could be without any income for a while. And I might not be able to obtain other employment to recover lost salary.

"Ana, we hope to have grandchildren in the future. They might need financial help for school and, eventually, college expenses. If I lose my job, then we would have to live off what money you make and from any odd jobs I can get. We will most likely have to tap our small savings account for living expenses. When I reach sixty-two, I will receive a modest social security check each month. That would leave little money for helping educate our grandchildren should they need it, or even for supporting ourselves."

I asked Ana before I left for school on Monday, "If I actively oppose the school board, can I afford to lose my job over a book? Should I take the chance? I would be sacrificing what I have built up for my family over a book. Is this all really worth it?"

Ana seldom got angry, but she was now. "Damn it, Mark! I realize you have given me the downside of speaking out. But since Ken Lewiston died, you have always asked, 'What would Ken do?' You didn't go to his service, much less speak at it. I believe you should have. You have never lived it down and I don't think you ever will until you stand up for what is right, which is what Ken would do.

"The rest of us will be alright, but you won't if you don't fight for what you believe is right. I can get a weekend job, and you could get a part-time or even a full-time job."

"I don't want you to have to do that," I said.

"I realize that. Mark," Ana replied. "Our kids will be just fine. But you won't if you shrink from doing what you know to be the right thing again. You will spend the rest of your life thinking about what you should have done. You will just wither away. I might wither with you, and our kids won't ever know what to do in the face of powerful people. We need to fight for what is right. Damn it, Mark. Fight!"

What Ana said upset me because I knew I had

buckled when Ken died. Ana must have talked to Joel because he called shortly after I finished talking with his mother.

"Dad, I know you have to get to school shortly," Joel said, "but I have one thing to say to you."

"What is that, son?"

"Do it!"

After receiving Joel's directive, Suzie called. I picked up the phone and without asking me how I was because she must have assumed that I knew why she was calling, she blurted, "Dad, do it. Fight!"

It was like a surprise party. I received one call after another—all part of a family conspiracy telling Dad what he needed to do for his well-being and in this case—his lasting conscience.

They had ganged up on me. In the minds of my wife, son, and daughter, I had to do what Ken would do, and what I should do regardless the consequences.

I did not tell Joel or Suzie that after talking with Ana I had already made up my mind. Their mother's conviction, coming from my best friend, wife, and reference point was enough for me. I had turned away when asked to speak at Ken's service, but there was going to be no shrinking from duty this time. I decided to stand and say what I should say even though I might be the only faculty voice defending Ms. J. and her use of the book.

On Monday morning, I took care of a couple of administrative tasks prior to meeting with my colleagues in the cafeteria. When I arrived, they were all there. We had limited time prior to teaching our respective classes.

Before anyone else could say anything, I stammered, "I am going to the board meeting tonight and I am going to defend Julia and her use of the book. I don't expect any of you to come or speak because of the risks involved. You have your jobs and families to think about and take care of, but I am well past mid-way in my career and will speak out. I should have done so earlier. I didn't. I will now."

Only Charles Yates responded. His face tightened. "Mark, are you sure you want to do this? You might lose your job and a lot more."

"Yes, Charles, thanks for your concern," I said, "but this is what I must do."

———

When I arrived in my first class, it was clear the students knew the board meeting involved censoring a book and Ms. J's job.

"Mr. M., what is going to happen tonight?" Janet asked as the class began.

"I do not know," I responded.

Another student asked, "Will Ms. J. be fired?"

"I don't know that either."

"Will you or any other Bailey High teachers get into trouble?"

"I don't know." I was unable to answer my students' questions. I wanted to, but I had no answers.

We proceeded to the lesson of the day. I tried to make the history as relevant as possible. We discussed Rosa Parks, Henry David Thoreau, Harriet Tubman, Cesar Chavez, Jane Addams, Martin Luther King Jr., Alice Paul, Mahatma Gandhi, and the many men and women arrested and jailed seeking suffrage. We talked about people who confronted authority in order to stand and speak.

The Board of Education set the meeting for 7 P.M. Ms. J. and the controversy over the book led the agenda. At seven o'clock sharp, the board president gaveled the meeting to order. Gorham's citizens had already packed the auditorium; late arrivals stood.

The first speaker against the book spoke, "We do not want such smut poisoning the minds of our children. The book must go and anyone who would use such a book must go too. This trash infects the minds of our children through its tolerant attitude and explicit advocacy of immorality. I say let's get this book out of our sight and send packing any teachers who support its use."

Following applause, the second speaker said, "I agree with everything the first speaker expressed. We should not in any way condone unnatural acts. Using the book in class gives sanction to homosexuality. And, for all we know, the teacher who is using the book is a homosexual too."

As soon as laughter stopped, Sharon Rosse took her turn. She had been a student in my class last year and was in Ms. J's this year. Sharon stood, and said, "We cannot learn if we do not explore new ideas and think about them. Ms. J. is great in getting us to think about new things. She presents many controversial ideas in class that come from literature. She allows us to arrive at our own conclusions. Please let Ms. J. stay as our teacher and let us read the book so we can learn to think for ourselves."

It was my turn to speak.

"I fully realize what I am doing tonight," I said. "I am in complete support of Ms. J. and her use of the book under question in her classes. I know the book is not on the approved list. However, I support what Bailey High student, Sharon Rosse, said about the book helping students learn to think for ourselves. This is something that we, as educators, are trying to help our students learn—how to think for themselves.

"Ms. J. is the kind of teacher who can help her students understand differing perspectives when they read contentious material. We owe this to our students, and we owe to ourselves the courage to teach about controversial subjects. I want to work in a school system that welcomes new ideas and is not afraid to discuss them. Therefore, I endorse the use of the book in Ms. J's classroom, and I support her as a teacher. Thank you for hearing what I have to say."

I heard some rustling of chairs and clapping behind me as I concluded. Returning to my chair, I saw my potluck group members standing together with thumbs up.

My colleagues and I, along with the rest of the audience in attendance at the school board meeting on that Monday evening, listened quietly and intently as the nine school board members split their vote five to four for keeping the book in the curriculum, and Julia Brack in her classroom.

During the first period the next morning, Ms. J.'s Bailey High students resumed reading and discussing the feared narrative.

Chapter 8: Daniel

We had not seen Ana's mother since she helped to deliver Joel in February of 1971. Each year we exchanged Christmas cards with Mom. Her greetings to us arrived either early or late—rarely on time—depending on when she could find a post office.

Mom also tried to send cards to Joel in celebration of his birth. The grandmother had spent meaningful birth time with her grandson. For Suzie, the child Mom never caressed or cuddled, she could only imagine the beauty. When she could, Mom sent birthday wishes to Suzie with words longing for the grandchild she yearned to embrace and never had.

We wanted to find Mom and be with her again. Every time we reached her by telephone, she was engrossed in her work assisting farm workers on the West Coast. Always moving from one place to another, Mom did not stay in one locale very long.

The demands of teaching and our activities with Joel and Suzie prevented us from leaving Gorham for the time necessary to trace Mom's whereabouts. Even though friends offered to care for our children, we did not feel comfortable leaving them with someone else for a week or so. Even if we could make the trip, we were not sure we would be able to reach Mom and see her. She migrated with farm workers from encampment to encampment, caring for everyone who needed her along the way. We never quite knew where she was.

What we did know was that Mom had returned to Texas after Joel's birth. She then journeyed to California to march with Cesar Chavez to battle for the rights of migrant workers—a challenging task for those with little political power.

Ana and I were constantly on the go, either with our jobs or our children's activities. Guilt saturated Ana because she had not been able to see her mother since those meaningful minutes when Joel was born. Then, on January 10, 1986, we received a letter. It jolted Ana.

Dear Mark and Ana:

By the time you receive this, I will be gone. I found out last month that I have cancer and do not have long to live. I was told I have been breathing too many bad chemicals over the years. I knew I might be doing that, but ministering to the farm workers was most important to me.

I want you to know that I love you very much as well as my beautiful Joel. I did not meet Suzie, but I know that she must be beautiful too. I love her too.

Ana, I know I have not been a good mother. I do not know why. I have only been with you one crucial time, and that was the birth of Joel. I feel bad for that being the only time. I put my life's work ahead of my family. I feel bad for that too.

My work in the fields, organizing and ministering, was of importance to me. I know that with Mark you are in good hands. I am sorry I have not been a good parent because you only had one. That, too, is my fault and I regret it.

A friend has helped me to write this letter to you. I want you to know that I have always loved you. I love Mark, Joel, and Suzie also. Please tell them that.

With God's help, I will watch over my family forever.

Love forever,

Your Mom

In our years of marriage, I seldom saw Ana cry. She had developed a steely façade during her childhood as friends came into her life and then vanished. When she read her mother's letter, tears flowed. Ana sobbed so loudly that Joel and Suzie stopped playing a card game and ran into the room. Our children were unaccustomed to seeing their mother distraught and weeping.

Ana repeated over and over, "I should have gone to my mother. I should have found her. I am so sorry I didn't."

It wasn't long after Mom's letter that we received a two-sentence letter informing us that Mom had passed. The writer expressed condolences but did not communicate much more. We later learned from a friend that Mom's burial took place in a field in California. We do not know where. Ana, with dogged determination, resolved to find out. "Someday, if not now," she declared, "we will locate her grave."

Shortly thereafter, another letter arrived in our mail box.

Dear Ana:

I know you do not know me or maybe that I even exist. I am your brother. Well, half-a-brother. We both have the same mother. I live in New Mexico. I found out about you when a friend of our mother's wrote to me telling me that our mother had died and that I had a sister in Massachusetts. I would like to meet you someday. I am thirty-five years old. How old are you? Please write to me when you can. I move around a lot, but you could write to me at General Delivery, Albuquerque, New Mexico. Oh, my name is Daniel and my last name is Garcia.

Love from your brother (half),

Daniel

After some of the shock wore off, Ana said, "Mark, I have to find him. I couldn't go to my mother. I did not know where she went when she left us after Joel's birth, where she was when she was dying, or where she is buried. I could not go to her because I could not find her. I must find Daniel, though. He may know more about Mom's life, her passing, and where she is buried."

"Ana," I said, "why don't you write him at the address in New Mexico and then we will decide what to do next."

"O. K. I will, but Mark," she said, "I have to find him."

Ana wrote to Daniel as fast as she could. We lived close enough to the post office to walk to drop off mail. Ana ran.

We did not hear from Daniel for two months, which alarmed Ana. Then on a Saturday in the spring of 1987, we heard tapping on the door.

I answered the door and the likeness was obvious. He did not have to tell me who he was. I said, "Your name is Daniel, isn't it?"

"How did you know?" Daniel appeared bewildered.

"The resemblance, Daniel. You look like your sister—my wife, Ana. And, my relatives via Ana, the Garcias," I explained. "You Garcias just show up. I love it. Please come in. Our home is the Garcias' home."

Daniel smiled whimsically. "I guess that all makes sense."

Ana was upstairs and came down the stairs after she heard the knock on the door. As soon as she saw her brother, she knew who he was. Ana let go a muffled scream, and then, "Oh, my God. Oh, my God. It is you. Daniel, Daniel, Daniel! It is you, Daniel. It is really you! Tell me, Daniel, that it is you."

As soon as Daniel saw Ana and heard her call his name, he whisked pass me.

Ana lunged into Daniel. She snatched him before he could reach her. I did not think she would ever release him. "You are Daniel, aren't you? You are. Tell me you are," Ana instructed.

"I am. Yes, yes, I am your brother," Daniel cried through Ana's taut clasp.

The newly-discovered brother's prolonged hug convinced Ana that it was, indeed, Daniel. "My brother, now that I have found you, I do not want to let you go—ever, ever, ever. Daniel, Daniel. How did you find me?" Ana asked, still holding her brother closely.

"How could I not find you?" he replied. "After Mom died, I received a letter from a friend of our mother's telling me about you and where you lived. Then I received your letter to me in Albuquerque, so I decided to find you. Ahha! Here I am!"

"Why didn't you call?"

"I wanted my arrival to be a surprise."

"It is! It is a wonderful surprise. Yes, yes, it is a surprise," Ana said, still in a state of shock. "I am so glad you found me. I mean, us. You must stay with us. Please."

"I will if it is okay."

"Of course it is. Yes. Please stay," I said. "We have an extra bed already made. We never know when Ana's kin will come to visit." I let out a laugh. "It must be the Garcia way. Your mother just showed up. The Garcias just appear. That way we don't have to wait for you to come; we don't have to worry or be apprehensive. You just turn up, like apparitions. We love it."

"Mark, it is okay isn't it?" Ana asked, still in disbelief that all of this was happening.

"Yes, of course it is. Daniel is a member of our family and must stay with us. Daniel, we are your family. If you wish to, please stay with us."

Ana and Daniel spent most of the rest of the day talking and holding hands. Daniel did not know much more about their Mom than Ana did. He could only guess where she was buried or who to contact to find out.

Ana introduced Daniel to his nephew, Joel, who had quietly joined us to find out what was going on. Daniel and Joel connected immediately. Daniel knew how to play. Joel, a teenager, had found a playmate and darted in and out of the house retrieving every ball he could find.

Joel dressed to go outdoors before Daniel could put his bags in Joel's room where he would sleep in the top bunk.

"I will get your bags into the room," I said. "So, go ahead outside with Joel to play catch."

Once she realized something was going on, Suzie traipsed downstairs. Ana introduced her to her uncle. Daniel and Suzie got to know each other quickly. Daniel's agile smile lighted the room, drawing Suzie to him. Ana and I marveled at Daniel's vivacious personality. He radiated charisma, immediately comforting his family.

As Daniel collected his niece and nephew around his six-foot frame, his muscular arms swept Joel and Suzie off their feet. Their chatter filled the house. They played outside until lunch was ready. Our children celebrated when their uncle morphed into a growling bear.

When they heard that lunch was ready, Daniel, Joel, and Suzie tumbled into the house, ripping their jackets off. Their spirited noise crackled through the kitchen. The joyful clamor continued when they sat down for peanut butter and jelly sandwiches. With Daniel now in our hearts, our family felt more complete.

—

Daniel was not with us for quite a month before there was an unwelcome rapping on the door. This time it was not a relative, which would have added another thrill. Instead, we were astonished when we found two Gorham police officers at our door.

The police were looking for "a guy named Daniel who is supposed to be living here. We would like to ask him some questions."

"What is this about, officers?" I asked.

"We are after illegal drugs and the pusher who is selling them to users," one of the officers explained. "We have some questions we want to ask."

The police lacked a warrant to search for narcotics, but they had detected the person they were looking for. They said they might be back. Gorham's version of the "drug squad" on our front steps shook Ana and me. School teachers in Gorham could do without the attention.

Soon after, Ana asked Daniel rhetorically, "You aren't involved in this drug business are you, Daniel?"

"No, of course not. When I was downtown Gorham

the other day, this guy asked me to hold a bag for him," Daniel explained. "I did not know that the bag had some marijuana in it. Someone must have seen me with the bag before the guy came back to get it. Now that I think about it, a bystander must have surmised what it was and then told the police that I had it in my hand.

"In some way, they found out who I was and where I live in town. So, they came to the house to check things out—that's all I can tell you because that is all there is. Ana, I promise. I am not into selling drugs. I use them recreationally now and then, but I have never sold them."

"Daniel, you have shown the kids that you have quite a bit of money with you. Now I am wondering: How do you get money?" Ana asked with doubt in her voice and fear in her eyes. "I know you always seem to have some money, and the kids have seen that you have a stash of cash with you at all times. So, where in the world did you get all that money?"

"Actually, I don't have that much money. I trick Joel and Suzie by putting a twenty-dollar bill over a bunch of George Washingtons, so it looks like I have a lot of cash. I don't. I have a little over fifty dollars. I had some odd jobs in the southwest, here and there. I saved some money when I worked at a steady job in Texas. I spent some cash getting here. Now that I have been here for a while and depleted the money I had, I don't have any more than what I just told you."

"Are you sure Daniel?" Ana pushed. "Are you telling us the truth? We must know to help you."

"I promise," he said. "I do not sell drugs."

"If the police come back, you are going to need a lawyer. You do not want to go to jail and we don't want you to go to jail," Ana continued, "and you don't need a misdemeanor or a felony on your record, especially one regarding drug trade. That would make it hard for you to get a job anywhere."

"Ana, I promise. I am telling you the truth," Daniel said. "Even though I have fifty or so dollars with me, I have some bills to pay. In fact, after I pay the bills, I will be broke. I don't have money for a lawyer."

"We will try to get a public defender then," I explained calmly. "Daniel, you will have to prove that you can't afford a lawyer."

"No problem, Mark. I can prove it because I don't have any money to pay for a lawyer."

"Well, proof will be necessary."

"But, Mark, are public defenders as good as a paid lawyer?" Ana asked. "Also, it is hard to prove a negative—that Daniel is NOT involved. I don't want my brother to be convicted of a crime. He could spend time in jail and come out a hardened criminal."

"Of course, I understand. We don't want any of that to happen," I said.

"And, Daniel, as I said, with a record you would then have trouble obtaining a job," Ana went on. "A conviction could stay on your record forever."

"I know Ana. You are frightening me with what you are saying. I am scared now," Daniel gagged through his words.

"I am sorry if I am upsetting you, but if the police are able to prove you had those drugs in your hands and then imply that you were planning to sell them, then how are you going to answer some tough questions in court?" Ana asked. "They might ask you: How did you get the drugs? Were you selling them? The prosecutor could try to get you to admit that you needed money to support your habit. These interrogators are good at getting defendants to say things you otherwise would not say. You will need a good defense attorney. Daniel, you are in a bundle of trouble. A plea deal would be bad enough. A conviction—worse."

The police did revisit. This time with a warrant. They searched our home and found a small amount of marijuana. Daniel was charged with "possession with intent to distribute." The case was scheduled to be heard in our county court. Since Daniel was able to prove that he could not afford to pay a lawyer, he was able to secure a public defender to help in his defense.

The courts in our county were crowded. With limited staff, the court processed more cases than they could promptly resolve. A magistrate took Daniel's case and reviewed the evidence.

The magistrate had multiple cases pending so she passed Daniel's case to her assistant. The magistrate's assistant also reviewed the evidence. She recommended that because the charge would be difficult to prove without a lengthy and expensive appeal the case be dropped. The prosecutor agreed.

Daniel had to pay court costs of $400. As the court official disposed of the case, she said, "I entrust you to your family. I understand that you can stay with them. I understand also that you have promised to help care for your cousins and provide a safe and nurturing environment for them. I hope I do not see you again in this setting on any more charges. Good luck, Mr. Garcia."

"Thank you, Your Honor," Daniel said. "I do not think you will see me again in this court."

"Mr. Garcia, you may go on your way now."

We thanked the public defender. As we were exiting the court house, Ana said, "Thank God for public defenders, especially this one. Otherwise, we would have had difficulty finding a lawyer we could afford, and then may not have gotten one as good as the public defender we had."

I wondered what happens to those accused of crimes who can't pay the court costs. I said to Ana, "If the accused can't afford a lawyer, how do they come up with the $400? What happens then?"

We thought it unjust that a person like Daniel, without money, would have to pay court costs, but that was what this court required. If Daniel stayed out of the legal system in the future, his record would remain clean. Ana and I scraped together enough to pay the costs for him. Daniel agreed that he would get a job and pay us back through helping with Joel and Suzie.

For three years in our home, Daniel imparted the best care, support, and companionship for our children we could have hoped for. By the end of the time that he lived with us, Daniel had pulled himself together, earned money by working part-time jobs, paid us back for the court costs, and saved enough money to travel to California.

In California, with our blessing, Daniel proposed to try to find Mom's trail to continue her life's work. He planned to minister, as his mother had, to farm workers as well as to their families. And, also like his mother, champion the human and civil rights of migrant workers.

Ana's last words to him were, "Daniel, please find out where our mother is buried, and, as soon as possible, please let me know where her grave is. I have to find it, and when I do, I want to go to pay my respects."

After Daniel left our home and said goodbye to us, Ana said to me, "Before Daniel came in to my life, I did not know I had a half-brother. At the end of his stay with us, I have a brother."

Daniel wrote to us after he joined the farm workers on the West Coast.

Dear Ana and Mark:

I am continuing the work our mom did. I am looking for where she has been laid to rest and will let you know as soon as I find her.

Also, I have begun studying laws that affect farm workers.

To help the workers and their families, I have decided to find a way to go back to school to earn a bachelor's degree. I hope to then go on to law school.

I want to spend the rest of my life on this earth doing the work Mom did—working with, advocating for, and defending those who toil in the fields.

I know how important it is to you, so I will keep looking for Mom's grave. When I find it, I will let you know.

Ana, I hope you and I can visit Mom together.

Sent with Love,

Daniel

Another letter arrived six months later. I opened the envelop, scanned the message, then read the notification to Ana.

Dear Mr. and Mrs. Blenchard:

We found your names, identities, and address in Mr. Daniel Garcia's wallet. We regret to inform you that Mr. Garcia was shot to death.

It was reported that he was killed when he attempted to stop a rape of a farm worker. The alleged perpetrator escaped and has not been arrested. Mr. Garcia's body has been cremated. We are sorry for your loss.

Chapter 9: Joel

"Mark, I wonder why Joel does not have a date for the prom," Ana said. "He doesn't seem to have any girlfriends. He has acquaintances who are girls, but he does not have girlfriends if you know what I mean. Everyone says he is good-looking. I don't understand why he doesn't have a girlfriend or even hang around with very many girls."

"Ana, I am not sure what you mean," I said. "What is it you are trying to say?"

"Joel is eighteen now and about to graduate from high school," she explained. "He has plenty of good friends, but they are almost all guys. Mark, you don't think he is...you know.... Do you?"

"Ana, I am a little slow now and then getting the point. However, I am beginning to get what you might be alluding to," I said. "I guess I know what you are trying to tell me, but I don't want to say the word. If what I think you might be trying to tell me is what you are trying to tell me then I just don't know, and I am not sure I want to hear it spoken out loud. Ana, I haven't really thought about Joel's lack of friends who happen to be girls. I am not sure I want to think about it either."

"Mark, I realize I may be beating around the bush,

but I do think we need to talk about it."

"WHY?"

"You don't have to get all upset, Mark," Ana said. "I do think we should talk to him about it—you know—the lack of girl friends? This whole thing is also upsetting to me."

"I am sorry I raised my voice and came at you. This issue is so unnerving," I said as my stomach churned. I was reminded of walking in the woods with Mrs. Bennett. I was getting that about-to-vomit feeling.

"Yes, this issue is unsettling. But, Mark, hiding from the truth doesn't help."

"You might be right, honey," I agreed. "Maybe I should know about Joel. I just don't want to know. I know this all sounds confusing, but I want to know—yet I don't want to know.

"This whole discussion is a very uncomfortable topic for me. When I learned that Ken Lewiston was gay, I wondered for a while whether there was something wrong with him. Maybe I need to grow up about this. I may have adopted the prejudices of society about homosexuality. Maybe we should brace ourselves for what we might hear. But why? What is wrong with it? Oh, damn, I do not know what I am saying. I am so confused."

"Maybe we both need to be more mature about this and stop dancing around the issue," she suggested. "And maybe we should not be so worried about what we might learn about Joel. It is his life, Mark. He should be able to live it the way he wants to and be who he is rather than adapting to what we and society think he should be."

"As parents, this is not easy for us to discuss. Even if I were willing to ask him, I am not sure how to approach a subject like that. And, I am still not certain I want to know the truth. You know what I mean. Don't you Ana?" I asked.

"Why would you not want to know the truth?" Ana asked. "Like you said, what is wrong with it? Really, Mark, what is wrong with it?"

"I don't know. I, like other males, grew up when people who were 'that way' stayed in the closet, or in hiding if you will," I tried to explain. "Things have changed. But if Joel is 'that way' then we may have to deal with it."

"Mark, PLEASE stop saying 'that way' as if there is something seriously wrong with Joel or anyone like him," Ana said.

"Maybe there is nothing wrong being gay, but I have always been told there is. I have come to believe it is okay for others, but not for my child," I said. "Now, I do not know. I do not know what to believe or think anymore."

"Mark, I don't think there is anything wrong with being gay. We, you and I, and our society need to be more adult and mature about differences," she pointed out. "Everyone is a human being and should be given and regarded with dignity. Some people are different— that's all!

"As his father, don't you believe we should let Joel live his life the way he wishes to do so? And, shouldn't we allow everyone else to live their lives the way they desire? Maybe we ought to encourage people to follow their own passions wherever they might lead. Just maybe we ought to do that."

When Joel graduated from high school, he asked Ana and me to sit down for a "talk" before he went off to college. He recognized we were uncertain about what he was doing with his life.

In the conversation, Joel never told us directly that he was gay. We said nothing other than, "Joel, we love you."

Our teenage son generally did not say much to us about anything. After our message of love, our son did give us a wily smile. We each hugged Joel. He responded with a pseudo-hug and air-kiss.

Joel graduated from Bailey High School and decided to enter a branch of the state university. In college, Joel joined as many student organizations he could find time for. He also wrote for the student newspaper during all four years as a college student.

By the time Joel finished college, he decided to follow his parents into education and become a teacher. Joel told us, "I plan to become a fourth-grade teacher. I hope to help every child reach their potential and to accept themselves for who they are. And, Mom and Dad, I plan to live my life like my Uncle Daniel—with courage— regardless the consequences."

Ana and I did not tell him what many aspiring teachers are told, "You won't make much money, and as a beginning teacher you could lose your job if you stand up and fight for your students and colleagues."

Instead, we told him what we felt to the depth of our souls: "Joel, our son, your mother and father could not be prouder of who you are and what you want to do with your life. We love you fully, completely, without reservation, and forever."

Shortly after graduating from college, Joel marched in a "LGBTQ Pride" event. An on-looker yelled epithets as arm-locked demonstrators strode. When Joel passed by, he looked toward the slanderer. The protester stepped into the procession and punched Joel, bloodying his nose.

Daniel Garcia's nephew kept marching.

Chapter 10: "Risk"

"Are the schools failing?" I asked our potluck group at the beginning of one of our Friday night dinners.

In 1983, President Ronald Reagan's eighteen-member National Commission on Excellence in Education released a clarion call for reform in the way the United States educated its youth. The report, titled, "A Nation at Risk: The Imperative for Educational Reform," included proposals intended to influence how educators teach, and how and what students learn. Warranted or not, the national report thrust educators toward uncharted paths during the 1980s.

The document's authors asserted that the United States was losing its economic advantage in the world, and, as a result, was falling behind other countries. The report ascertained the educational system in the United States required reform to make the United States more competitive economically among other nations.

"A Nation at Risk" boosted the growing obsession with standardized testing through comparing students within the United States with those around the world. The evidence at the time indicated that the United States possessed the world's most vibrant economy, had the strongest military, and its school system's compulsory education requirement provided funding for its public schools.

"Risk's" primary conclusion was that American public schools were failing to adequately educate its children in an increasingly interconnected world. Therefore, if it could be demonstrated that the schools were failing to compete, which the report maintained, then there was reason to alter the federal education system.

The activists' advocacy for change and how radical the changes would be depended on how badly the reformers believed the schools were performing, and how well the report could persuade the public that significant change was necessary. Thus, the "A Nation at Risk" report endorsed major restructuring in the educational system in the United States.

In 1980, Ronald Reagan, the former governor of California, had defeated the incumbent president, Democrat Jimmy Carter. As with almost any new president, President Reagan's administration promoted an agenda for reforming government and its institutions. One part of the plan was to transform the public schools in the country through "privatization."

The "A Nation at Risk" document stirred educators to discuss the report's implications during the ensuing years. After the ramifications of the report fully set in, Ana and I arranged a potluck Friday dinner meeting in October of 1987.

By the potluck date, most of us had learned during professional meetings and workshops about the recommended changes on restructuring the schools. Our group was ready to examine issues of what this all meant for teachers and students. The potluck diners included John Browne, Karla Betts, Charles Yates, Cheryl Wattsen, Jake Spanner, April Danniels, Megan

Straffa, Claudia Pace, Zack Barber, Ana and me.

Zack Barber, who read and supported the reforms, reported to the dinner group, "The Reagan administration contends reform can be accomplished through providing more choice. The concept of education choice aims to furnish families with publicly funded vouchers, so they can choose the school they believe will offer the best education for their children. By using the vouchers as if they are cashier-checks, families choose their schools, and remit tuition fees using publicly funded vouchers to pay enrollment and tuition costs.

"In some states, public money could be used to pay for a religious education which I agree raises First Amendment concerns. However, in general I am in support of what the Reagan administration wants to do in education. I believe students and parents choosing their educational institutions is essential for a free society."

"I hear what you are saying, Zack," I said, "but is our nation at risk because of what we have been doing or maybe what we are not doing in our schools?"

"We are failing because of what we are not doing. Our schools are failing and putting our nation at risk. We are now behind some other countries in international test scores. The rest of the world is passing us by. We need to improve our schools, and do so fast," Charles said.

Cheryl Wattsen added, "I agree with what Charles and Zack have said. We are behind other nations economically. As the report maintains, it could hurt our national security and put our nation at risk. We need to reform our schools to create a more competitive educational system."

Megan Straffa countered, "I disagree with Charles, Cheryl and Zack. We have never been ranked very high in the world educationally, and we certainly have never been number one. How could we have been falling behind when we have never been ahead? Studies put us somewhere in the middle of the pack.

"The reformist's 'falling behind' allegation is premise number one in the anti-public-school agenda. The argument goes: 'The public schools are failing; ergo, they need to be changed.' Well, if the truth is that the public schools are not failing because we have never been ahead, then the privatization-reform argument falls apart. Besides, none of these studies factor in that we educate everyone in a highly diverse population and many other countries don't.

"If I need to remind anyone, our top students are among the best in the world. In fact, students here in Massachusetts score as high as any country on international tests. The real challenge is to create schools to ensure everyone is a top student. I believe we can do that."

"But, Megan," Charles retorted, "we should be number one. Look how much money we spend. We get very little for the large proportion of our local, state, and federal budgets that we spend on education, and your proposal that everyone can be a top student is pie in the sky stuff."

Karla joined the discussion, "The difference, Charles, is that our educational system tries to educate everyone. Since Public Law 94-142 in 1975, we have attempted to provide a public education in the least restrictive environment for all. I don't believe other countries do this, and to our credit, we attempt to provide an education for everyone. We look out for children with special needs, and we should.

"I believe the United States strives to educate everyone to their full potential. The evidence shows that we are one of the few educational systems in the world that aims to educate everyone regardless students' circumstances. My art classes, for example, are a place for everyone to be special. We don't worry about being number one. We just aim to be creative. This is extraordinary and exceeds any average anyone can come up with. In fact, each of my students is beyond average because the act of creating is itself exceptional."

Cheryl added, "You have to admit, Karla, we have some work to do in our educational institutions. We spend a lot of our national treasure on schooling. And, according to this report, we don't get much quality education for the large amount of money we spend."

"That is if you agree with the report. Yes, Cheryl," Megan said, "I agree we have some work to do. What we do, however, depends on what we think the problem is. We can always improve, but is the 'Risk' report helpful in what it calls for us to do—more testing and so forth?"

Zack rejoined the discussion, "If the problem is that the schools are failing because we are not doing a good job educating, then I believe the solution is different than what Megan is advocating. She is arguing that the problem is a lack of resources, and that we would do even better in educating every student if we have more economic support."

Jake said, "Yes, Zack, I agree with your summary of your respective positions. I would like to add though that the Reagan administration is conservative, so they are looking for a conservative solution—less money. Furthermore, they don't like unions and they are against the unions' alleged hold they are said to have on the public schools. And, I mean alleged. If the Reagan administration can weaken the public schools, they can weaken the unions. I believe the problem is that we need to fight back against the status quo.

Maybe a stronger union will enable us to do that, and, if additional resources are needed, which I believe they are, then a strong union can help us attain them."

"That is pretty naive, don't you think, Jake?" Cheryl asked.

"No, Cheryl, I don't think I am being naïve," Jake argued. "I think it is entirely possible. We need to know how the political system works. It responds to power, and a formidable union would be able to apply the necessary pressure to get action in our favor. Politicians play hard ball. We need political power too. The people who are in control want to weaken unions. Then they wouldn't have teachers' advocates to contend with. Without a potent union, they can push us around. It is that way in Gorham and elsewhere in the country. I believe that strongly."

"I get your point, Jake," I said. "What then should our response be to the call for reform? And, what do the rest of you advocate—I mean those of you are arguing that our problem is a lack of resources?"

"I continue to disagree, Mark, that resources are the issue. It is not a lack of resources. What we as educators need to do is improve. It is as simple as that. We need to improve. We need to teach better so students will learn," Charles said.

"Yes. I support Charles on that. We need to stop whining. Do our job. Improve our practices; improve our teaching," Cheryl said."

"As she frequently does, Cheryl agrees with me. She is intelligent and can figure things out for herself and not believe the pro-union propaganda you liberals spout. So, thanks, Cheryl," Charles said. "All these liberals seldom agree with me, but you do at some crucial times and this is one of them. Maybe it is because you are an English teacher and use logic. We social studies teachers sometimes employ fuzzy thinking."

"Oh, come on, Charles," Megan said. "Are you trying to divide the group along subject matter lines?"

"As usual, Megan, the truth hurts, doesn't it?" Charles responded.

"Hey, everyone, let's get back to the problem of what to do about the 'Risk' report," I said.

"Okay, Mark, but how will we do all the things we need to do as teachers without resources?" Megan asked.

"But, Megan, as I said, we have enough resources," Charles argued. "So, if we just do our jobs, then students will learn. It is that simple. To cite William of Ockham, the simple solution with the fewest variables is frequently the best."

"Oh, come on, Charles, you are trying to show off," Megan complained.

"Sorry, Megan," Charles snapped. "I was just trying to throw a little intellect at you, the medieval philosopher's tenet advocating the simplest hypothesis with the fewest variables was known as 'Ockham's razor.' It cuts through the maize and smoke and mirrors and cuts your argument to threads."

"Oh, Charles, this is so typical of you. You are trying to be so erudite, and it is coming across as one-ups-man-ship. And, in your case it never quite works," Megan said.

John Browne added, "I don't think you are right on this one, Charles. Forget all the Ockham stuff. Poverty is a big factor as well as its resulting effects. If we had less poverty, I contend that our schools and the students in them would do better. It is not as simple as you have argued it is, Charles."

"I concur with John on that. It is not that simple," Jake said.

"I agree with both John and Jake on this," Megan

interjected. "We need more resources to combat the pervasive effects of poverty in the lives of some of our kids. Without the resources, the kids from low-income families really don't have a chance. I think the complexity of the issue bypasses the simplistic, conservative argument."

"I concur with what you just said, Megan," Jake said, "and I don't think privatizing is the answer. What are we going to do? Are we going to let fast food restaurants and oil companies run schools? As others have said— it is much more complicated than the easy solutions Charles and Cheryl are promoting."

"Sorry, Jake, your argument is absurd. Here you liberals go again," Charles argued. "You are exaggerating what could happen. Once again, you are fear-mongering, and, Jake, how do you know that privatization does not and will not work?"

"Damn it, Charles, I don't think I am fear-mongering or exaggerating. Powerful private companies are ready and willing to take over the schools through using vouchers and other ways to privatize," Jake explained. "They see education as a new cash cow, so they can make profits through tapping the public's coffers and using vouchers for private schools run by private corporations not accountable to the public. And your other question was…?"

"How do you know privatization doesn't work? Jake, it hasn't really been attempted yet," Charles pointed out.

"Charles, I know privatization does not work," Jake said. "There is lot of research supporting my contention that private schools, when controlling for income, are no more effective than public schools, and in some cases not as effective."

"Once again, you liberals are ganging up on the

one conservative in the room," Charles countered. "Although, Cheryl seems to understand."

"I may not be as conservative as you are, Charles, but I agree with the 'Risk' report. We are failing our students. Vouchers may help by providing parents and students with the ability to find schools that work for them. So, why not try them out? Maybe they will make a difference," Cheryl stated.

"By the way, Charles, we are not all liberals or conservatives. I am a Libertarian lest you forget. If I could, I would get rid of all the public schools," Zack piped up. "I wouldn't privatize them. I would just eliminate them."

"Zack, you are being hypocritical again. You get your paycheck through working in a public school," Jake declared.

"Jake, I realize that. As I have said in previous discussions, I like eating and supporting my family. Besides, I enjoy teaching and coaching basketball. I believe I earn the check I receive every two weeks," Zack said.

"Well, Charles, then in your opinion what is the 'Risk' report really all about?" John asked.

"If you are willing to listen, I will tell you."

"Charles, I am listening—carefully!" John responded.

"We are all listening, Charles," I said.

"The report clearly communicates that we are losing the economic advantages we have had since World War II, and that the problem lies within public schools. We are not doing the government-mandated job of educating students for the future. Therefore, we are losing out," Charles explained.

"If we are 'losing out' to the world as you say, Charles, then what do you or anyone else recommend we do about the problem?" John asked.

"In addition to what John just said," Megan added, "if, in fact, we have a significant problem in our educational system, which I most definitely think we do not, I would say it is our failure in getting students to think critically. I believe we do not teach students how to become critical consumers of the information they receive, but we should. I don't think we are at 'risk' in the world except when it comes to helping students think. Then maybe we would have something to teach the rest of the world, rather than the rest of the world teaching us something."

"Well, Megan, I think you are wrong AGAIN," Charles said. "We need to change just about everything about education. We need more standardized tests, so we can measure ourselves against other schools, states, and nations. Then we would know what to change."

"As I said, Charles, you are assuming we are failing and need to change. I don't believe that is the case. See, everyone, I don't accept the premise that the schools are failing. Therefore, my suggestions for what schools need to do to improve would be quite different than, say, the recommendations Charles and Cheryl have made. Also, I think Zack is wrong about there being enough resources."

"One way to find out if the schools are failing, Megan, is through standardized testing, but you don't want to do that. Do you?" Charles claimed.

"No, I don't Charles. No, I don't!" Megan exclaimed.

"Standardized testing works against some of the kids who are in my art classes," Karla stated. "My students are different, and I mean good different. My students defy standardization. In fact, great art is non-standard. So, standardization works against my students and works against what I try to do in the classroom. I help students express their creativity and live outside the standardized testing box; standard and creative is a contradiction in terms."

"And, in addition to what Karla just said," John added, "standardized testing also works against students from different cultures, especially minority cultures. By definition, standardized testing is for standardized students and results in standardizing students to the lowest standardized formula—not a good idea in my opinion."

"But standardized tests tell us something about students' language competence in writing and understanding English," Cheryl declared.

"Well, Cheryl, that is precisely the problem. It allows for only one way of writing English—the standard way. It does not provide for creativity or cultural differences," Megan said.

Cheryl countered, "I think you are wrong about that. I have been teaching English now for a while. If a writer knows the standard way of doing things, then one can deviate from the norm and do some creative writing."

"I have heard what you have all said," I declared. "There appear to be advantages and disadvantages to the changes the 'Risk' reformers recommend. What, then, should we do as educators? The national government has proposed reforms for a problem some of us do not think exists. While others in our group believe the lack of educational progress in our schools has placed our nation at risk—economically at least.

"In the midst of our impasse, I look forward to returning to school on Monday. At least, I think I do," I said.

Chapter 11: Lacey

"Who is the new classroom 'babe,' Mr. M.?" When I shopped for groceries in Gorham, or watched an athletic event off school grounds, students asked me the "babe" question. They surmised it must be okay to do so when they bumped into me off Bailey High School property.

Students in the school building or on the grounds would not refer to a teacher as a "babe" if they thought a teacher could hear a colleague so branded. If overheard in school, such language about a teacher would be deemed taboo.

Upon hearing a student make the comment while I was shopping for groceries, I knew who he was talking about. It was Lacey Walsh, a new teacher at Bailey.

The student added as I tried to remain expressionless in the check-out line, "You have to admit, Mr. M., she sizzles."

Ms. L. had made an impression.

After a decade or so without population growth, the Gorham, Massachusetts, school district grew in population in the mid-1980s. The increase in students followed a slight decrease in Gorham in the early 1970s.

The "baby boomers' boom" was having an impact.

In addition, some of the surrounding neighborhoods asked to join the Gorham system. When annexation was granted, the school system's enrollment grew even further. This growth necessitated hiring additional teachers to serve the expanding number of students at Bailey High.

With the Bailey High School enrollment swelling, Cheryl Wattsen, who was now chair of the English department, and I gained a teaching position to share between our departments.

The position required teaching two courses in each department and serving as a soccer team coach. The new teacher would be assigned to teach social studies and design innovative media literacy courses, an increasingly important field of study in the late 1980s. Cheryl and I planned to jointly interview applicants for the shared position.

After combing through the candidates' applications for the teaching position at Bailey High, we decided to interview Lacey Walsh as a potential faculty member.

Lacey had worked in the television industry for over a decade. She made more money as an on-air reporter than she ever would as a high school teacher. Yet, she applied for an open teaching position at Bailey High. This perplexed both Cheryl and me.

"Why would someone in the television industry with all its perks, including a high salary, want to teach high school students?" I asked Cheryl. "Why do you think Lacey Walsh wants to become a teacher at Bailey T. S. Memorial High School?"

"Mark, it beats me. However, if she wants to become a high school teacher and knows what she is getting into," Cheryl said, "Lacey's intriguing background and 'real world' experience would help us fill a void in our curriculum."

When we interviewed Lacey for the joint position, Cheryl began by asking Lacey the obvious question. "Lacey, why do you want to become a teacher?"

"First, let me say, thank you for giving me the chance to interview for this teaching position. I am very interested in the position. That is why I am here," Lacey responded.

"We are glad you are interested, Lacey," Cheryl said. "So, what attracts you to teaching with us here at Bailey High?"

"I appreciate the question, Cheryl," Lacey said with a smile. "I have multiple reasons for wanting to change professions and become a teacher. Should I go through them all?"

When Lacey asked us if we wanted to hear her reasons for wanting to teach, I recalled my own interview for a job in the Gorham school district. When the interviewer talked, I listened.

"Yes, Lacey," I said. "We are interested in why you want to become a teacher. So, go ahead, please. Take your time. We are listening."

"Foremost," Lacey began, "it is important for me to say upfront that I realize my responses may sound cynical, but I think if I provide candid answers you will see why I want to get out of the television industry and into teaching.

"As a teacher, I want to enable my students to read the increasingly technologically-advanced media, which is the field where I have the most experience. When the students comprehend how the various media really do their work, then they will see why learning media literacy concepts and skills are important in acquiring knowledge in English and social studies, as well as in other subjects."

"So, Lacey, how would you explain the process of

television programming to students in a way that is useful and essential for their educations?" I asked.

"Well, Mark and Cheryl, this is complicated," she explained, "because what I want to convey to students may sound overwhelmingly negative and lead to cynicism. I would communicate to students that it is important to remember that I have worked with some good correspondents who just want to inform the public, and that a number of them still want to do a good job at informing us. However, and here is the cynical part, in order to stay employed in the television business one must play the game."

"What game was that?" Cheryl asked.

"I will try to explain as best I can."

"Please do, Lacey," I said. "Along with your reasons for wanting to leave the television industry to teach high school students, we need to learn some of what you learned from TV work. We can then include the relevant units in our classes."

"Okay. First, I will tell you why I wanted to leave the television industry which should help me illustrate what I have to teach students.

"So, Cheryl and Mark, here goes—I realize this may sound trite, but my blonde hair fit well in an industry that values looks over knowledge and ahead of almost anything else, except, of course, profits."

"Yikes," I said. "In the past, I have assumed what you are saying to be the case but hearing it directly from a participant—a primary source—is startling."

"Yes, Mark, I believe in imparting to anyone who will listen that making money by looking good was and is commercial television's primary objective.

"The producers determined that I attracted viewers, so along with the owners and stockholders, I made money too. Thus, Mark and Cheryl, I got sick and tired of being exploited and in exploiting audiences for corporate dollars. As a result, as an educator—teaching truth to power has become attractive to me."

"Go on, Lacey, tell us more about how you attracted viewers," Cheryl coaxed.

"Well, Cheryl, in addition to the blondness, I and my on-air colleagues just couldn't be too thin. So, it helped if a television personality was petite and blonde. If you weren't naturally blonde, it was necessary to look as if you were. And, if you were not blonde or could not be made to look blonde then you needed other features to attract viewers, because that was what it was all about— attracting viewers—which attracted commercials, which made the broadcasters more profits. I believe you get the point," Lacey said.

"We do, Lacey. I believe we do. Please keep going," I said.

"Okay. Also, a woman on television couldn't be too old or show the aging process," Lacey continued. "The wrinkles had to go. Guys could have that older, gravitas look, but it was a 'no-no' for women to 'look' old. Attracting the male demographic was important, so females showing age was not a good way to stay employed. Of course, there are some exceptions but not many.

"I discovered that television news is a 'meat market' and I was the fillet. Flat stomachs were a must, and God forbid if a female television reporter had a 'baby bump' or prematurely aged on the job.

"Of course, men don't have baby bumps. If a woman had a child and showed a 'baby bump,' she was expected to flatten it out. No one ever said anything directly to the mothers, but it didn't take a genius to figure it out. It was 'body-shaming' on steroids.

"My blood boiled when harried mothers, showing

their motherhood, were coaxed into another role on the network so they wouldn't be seen. In addition, mothers had a 'double whammy' working against them. If someone birthed a child, then some managers started to doubt their commitment to the job. Childless bosses questioned an employee's priorities. They did so tacitly of course, but the message got through. Of course, male bosses didn't have to worry about such things."

"Geesus, Lacey," I said. "So, people were just reassigned if they didn't look the RIGHT way. Is that the way it happened?"

"Yah. That is the way it worked. Any question to management about the 'why' of the reassignment was met with babbling denial, distraction, or silence. The silence sent the message. Management had its ways of insulting non-verbally; a look of disparagement was enough to get the message across. And if you needed the job, you took the shove. There was no such thing as resistance.

"As a result of the obligatory 'right look' culture, unless a woman keeps looking good, their days on television are limited," Lacey explained. "I am not a natural blonde, but I needed to look like one, and as a woman gets older, her hairdresser is her best friend. However, even the hairdresser can't conceal the years and wrinkles. In some cases, the stylist may be able to hide and cover the gray or—God forbid—the white.

"Furthermore, Mark and Cheryl, some men on television grow their stomach size as time goes on, but they usually get a pass on their weight gain, because their bosses, who are usually men, 'understand.' Not all bosses understand, of course, but males have more latitude than females. Besides, with a well-tailored sport coat, men can hide an expanded middle. Women with extended middles are generally cast off the television set. A few extra pounds get you reassigned to a desk job or out in the field chasing ambulances. The perennial TV slogan, 'If it bleeds—it leads' prevails, and if they can't find the dramatic in the news then they are let go, or metaphorically hurled into in some back office." Lacey paused. "Should I go on?"

I nodded my head as Cheryl said, "Please do. I find your response important, and I believe I understand what you are saying. I don't like what you are telling us because it confirms my already skeptical beliefs about the television news industry, but we have to hear what happens behind the scenes and teach our students about why they are seeing what they are seeing on television. However, I believe the newspaper industry is different."

"Yes. The newspaper industry is quite different—a reporter's looks don't matter," Lacey explained. "The knowledge a reader can gain through reading is much more substantial than looking at a television screen. In addition, the reader is in control when reading whereas the programmer controls what we see on TV."

"I agree, Lacey. As an English teacher, I communicate to my students that the active act of reading is quite different from passive viewing," Cheryl said. "As you indicated, a reader is in control of the act, whereas the programmer controls you when you watch television—big difference."

"Cheryl, indeed, just looking at a screen is quite a different experience than reading a page where you have to think to obtain the information. Even reading 'trash' requires at least a minimal amount of thought. Watching television does not require any thought, just a comfortable sofa and a bevy of snacks.

"Furthermore, Cheryl and Mark, in the television business—which is all about watching and consuming— my Q-Ratings were all important to my bosses."

"What are Q-ratings?" I asked.

"Q-ratings measure a reporter's likability and drawing power on the screen," Lacey said. Basically, it tells your bosses whether viewers want to watch you. My employers found the scores important. If they were high, it meant I appealed to viewers which the bosses liked.

"Because it was called news, the male demographic watching us was of prime importance. I was told, 'Lacey, it is your lips that attract men to watch.' They have the money to spend on the advertised products."

"I don't get it, Lacey. Why your lips?" I said.

"Mark, you continue to be way too innocent in the ways of the world. I will explain it to you later in private," Cheryl said.

"I still don't get it, but I guess I will when you tell me later."

"Yes. Mark, I will tell you during lunch period," Cheryl said. "As you were saying, Lacey."

"You see, the theory was, if the male demographic watched then they would buy what was featured which was the ultimate objective of the programming," Lacey continued. "Those of us on television herded viewers into the program, readying the on-lookers for the commercials. I was the 'eye candy' attracting viewers to the products advertisers want to sell.

"The station's executives paid me well as wallpaper to deliver news through a screen. As I 'hooked' viewers, the 'bait'—me—made money, received the goodies associated with being thought of as a star, and I kept my well-paying job.

"Sounds cynical doesn't it? Well, it was the real world and still is. Commercial television is about the m's— money, money, and more money.

"Therefore, to summarize my reasons for teaching—I

116

want to teach at Bailey High, so my students will understand how the various print and visual media work, why they work that way, and how we can all become more media literate."

Chapter 12: Claude

Claude Ruzzio took my freshman World History class, and as a senior enrolled in my United States history since 1865 course. After I first had him in class, Claude showed significant improvement. He maintained his grades, keeping him on track to become the first in his family to complete high school.

Jason Burro and other Bailey High students from similar low-income economic backgrounds had succeeded in high school and some had graduated from college. Several faculty believed Claude could gain admission to college and succeed as a student. We thought, however, he would need financial aid and academic support to succeed in an institution of higher education.

I explained to Ana, "In most of the colleges Claude hopes to apply to, financial aid merit awards go to those who score well on standardized tests. Claude has earned solid grades, but because of test anxiety he panics when taking high-stakes tests and does not score well. Because of low test scores, he has been unable to gain enough scholarship support to make it to college. He just doesn't have the monetary backing to make it without financial assistance."

"Is there anything that can be done about his anxiety

when taking standardized tests?" Ana asked.

"Unfortunately, not much," I said. "Many of the students who receive high scores on standardized tests come from families that can afford tutoring. The knowledge of what to expect and how to handle it enables students to be less anxious. Test preparation helps those who can afford the assistance. The coaching provides a distinct advantage."

"Honey, that does not seem fair," Ana said.

"It isn't. The students from wealthier families have a step up on students like Claude who do not have the money to purchase the assistance," I continued. "In addition, the families of those students who receive the private tutoring are generally financially able to pay the student's tuition without scholarships from the college or aid from government agencies. Claude, on the other hand, can't afford the tutoring, yet needs the financial support high standardized test scores could provide him."

"So, Mark, are you saying that families with financial means can afford SAT coaching, and then, because of the assistance, their high scores on standardized tests can lead to "merit" scholarships they don't need?" Ana asked.

"Yes. That is what I am saying. In many instances that is the case. The rich get richer through higher education's "the-higher-the-income" reward system," I explained. "The college admissions departments argue that they try to recruit lower-income students. However, creating an equitable system has proved elusive."

"Maybe Bailey High could help pay for the test preparation course," Ana offered, "or maybe you and I could help Claude in some way."

"Honey, the school does not have the budget for one student never mind all the students who would be in line for help. And, as far as us helping, Claude has made it clear his mother does not accept anything she believes is charity. It would have to be a gift and that gets complicated when a teacher gives money to a student."

"Mark, does she have a husband or relative who could help?"

"Unfortunately, her husband died one year after their marriage. He died late in the pregnancy. So, there does not seem to be a source of money anywhere."

"Do you know anything about her background?" Ana inquired.

"After the death of her husband, she moved with Claude into her mother's small apartment in Florida."

"What happened then?"

"Well, Ana, it didn't get any better," I explained. "Shortly after Claude's birth, Marylyn Ruzzio's mother died."

"Ouch. It seems Mrs. Ruzzio did not have much hope for the future," Ana said. "What did she do?"

"She had to hustle to find a job with a living wage to support her and her son. Her mother's sister lived here in Massachusetts, so Mrs. Ruzzio moved in with her aunt in a two-bedroom rental. That way Claude could attend school here in Gorham."

"So, what has happened with Claude and his mother since moving to town?"

"As soon as she arrived in Gorham, Marylyn Ruzzio sought employment as a means to a decent life for her and Claude," I said.

Ana asked, "What kind of work was she able to get?"

"She waits tables at the Gorham Town Diner," I said. "Claude told me his mother loves the work."

"Do you know anything about what his father was like?"

"No, not really," I admitted. "I know very little. The way I understand it is that his father died shortly before his birth. Claude only knows his father through his mother."

Marylyn Ruzzio kept the Mrs. because she loved her husband and the son they had together. Mrs. Ruzzio wanted Claude to know that his father lived on in his son. She said to all who would listen, "I do not plan to ever marry again. I could never love anyone as much as I did and still love my husband, Claude's father. I will be Mrs. Ruzzio forever."

With the exception of Mrs. Ruzzio's aunt, Mrs. Ruzzio and her son did not have any other relatives in the area. On back to school night or around Gorham, other than occasionally being accompanied by her aunt, Mrs. Ruzzio traveled without a companion. When she visited the school to see how Claude was doing, Marylyn Ruzzio came and left alone.

Claude struggled academically at Bailey High. However, with a little help, Claude passed his courses with mostly B's and an occasional A in courses that interested him. Through his hard work, he advanced toward high school graduation as the first in his family to do so. Graduating from high school mattered to him, to the faculty, and especially to his mother. That was the good news.

When Claude realized that he was going to graduate, he came to see me. He was ecstatic, beaming with pride. Claude said, "Mr. M., I am going to graduate. I will be the first in my family to graduate from high school. I don't know many family members, but maybe me graduating will be an example for others." With tears in his eyes, his voice breaking, he said, "I wish my dad could be there in person for my graduation. My faith, though, tells me he will be watching from heaven because I know he is there."

Claude recognized that graduating from high school was a significant accomplishment. He had worked hard and deserved the diploma he was about to receive. As another first for his family, Claude aspired to attend college.

Bailey High's graduation was scheduled for Monday, June 17, at 7 o'clock. Claude's mother was slated to work that day and evening. She planned to take the time off so she could attend the graduation. She yearned to see her son walk across the dais to collect his diploma. Mrs. Ruzzio earned just enough money working as a waitress to pay the bills to house and feed herself and her son. She could ill afford the loss of a night's pay.

Marylyn Ruzzio anticipated trading shifts with another waiter so she could attend graduation ceremonies without the loss of income. However, the plan to attend her son's graduation fell through when the waiter who could have covered for her became ill. Mrs. Ruzzio frequently covered for others, so they would not miss a day's pay. No one else was available, and Mrs. Ruzzio refused to plead for a night off resulting in overloading the diner staff.

I told Ana, "Claude's mother simply cannot afford the loss of an evening's pay. If another substitute who would trade shifts and share with her cannot be found, there would be no pay for that day. I hope something can be worked out, so this hard-working, dedicated mother can see her son receive his high school diploma."

"Mark, something has to be worked out," Ana agreed. "This is a one-time event for Claude and his mother."

"I know, Ana. I know. When he heard the news that his mother might not be there for his graduation, Claude was devastated. He said he understood, but it was clear to me that he was deeply disappointed. Claude has worked diligently to earn his diploma and wants his mother to see him march across the stage," I said.

Claude's heart had already broken by the time he reported to me that his mother could not be at his graduation. So, when I saw Claude in school, I told him, "The faculty members will be there to see you get your diploma."

Claude responded, "Mr. M., that is great. I appreciate you will all be there, but it won't be the same without my mom at my graduation."

Karla, who had Claude in her art class, found him in tears shortly after he had heard that his mother could not get off from work on graduation night. In a telephone call, Mrs. Ruzzio told Karla, "I cannot afford to lose a day's pay. Ms. K., I can't afford that. When I cover for another waiter, I give the tip money to them and then my substitute does the same for me when I cannot work. This time, there is no one available to cover me. I have too many bills to pay. And, I do not want anyone to just give me money. I won't accept charity or go on welfare to pay my bills. I am too proud for that. I told my husband before he died that I would find a way to take care of Claude on my own. It is a sacred promise I made to Claude's father I cannot break."

Karla, as was her custom, felt deeply for the student and now his mother. Her voice shook as she told me, "Mark, no one in his family will be there for Claude." She followed asking, "Is there any way we can get Claude's mother to the graduation?"

Ana and I quickly convened a potluck dinner. At the very least, we wanted to help his mother arrange a graduation party for Claude either before or after the graduation when she could attend.

Mrs. Ruzzio did not have much money to pay for party extras, but the faculty could pitch in for balloons, a present or two, and some food. We also wanted to see if we could find some way to get Claude's mother to the graduation. Ana and I said, "There has to be a way."

As we sat around at our impromptu potluck, I asked, "Okay, what can we do? Can we arrange a party for Claude and any other students who can come? We can honor them all, can't we? And if we brainstorm, maybe there is a way to get Mrs. Ruzzio to the graduation."

Charles was the kind of person and teacher who would do anything for any student he thought was working hard. Claude was one of those. Charles offered, "For the party I will get the balloons. I will get so many that it will be festive—red, white and blue. I will decorate every part of the outside of the house."

"Don't go overboard Charles," I said in jest. Charles' tendency was to go big when he got excited.

"Oh, come on Mark—you party-pooper."

"Alright, Charles, maybe a little overboard, or maybe even a lot overboard," I said. "Claude and his mother will certainly appreciate a multi-colored and vibrant celebration."

"Charles, could you add black balloons?" Megan asked. "The red, white, and blue are fine, but the school colors are red, white, and black, so I say add the black."

"Sure. I can do that. See, Megan, I do listen to your suggestions now and then," Charles said.

"I will make a cake," John volunteered.

"I call the ice cream," Claudia said.

"Yah, Claudia, you get the ice cream but make sure there is some for the rest of us," John said as we joined in the laughter.

"Chocolate. No nuts. I'm allergic," Jake directed.

"Let's find a way to decorate Mrs. Ruzzio's apartment and Claude's bedroom," Cheryl said. "I will check with his mother and her landlord to make sure all of the decorating is okay."

"Hey, everyone, here is an idea that might work. I used to wait tables and should be able to learn the diner's system relatively quickly," April Danniels explained. "Maybe the manager will let me work Mrs. Ruzzio's shift, then Mrs. Ruzzio could attend the graduation. I usually don't go to high school graduations anyway unless I know someone who is graduating, and I don't this year. Substituting for Mrs. Ruzzio is worth a try. Besides, maybe they will hire me permanently if I do a good job during the try-out," April Danniels half-joked.

"That may be worth a try, April. As an elementary school teacher, you don't have to be at the high school graduation. We will be there, and we need to get Claude's mother there," I said.

We had a plan.

On graduation day, the seniors lined up in their red, black, and white gowns. Claude Ruzzio's five-foot-two frame stood erect among the graduates. In the gymnasium's stands, Marylyn Ruzzio stood waving— tears sprinkling her cheeks. Standing aside Mrs. Ruzzio, Karla Betts and Charles Yates shared tissues.

Substitute waitress, April Danniels, gathered forty-five dollars in tips on graduation night. April even secured a part-time summer job in the diner.

When she returned to work a day after watching her son accept his high school diploma, Mrs. Ruzzio sighted gratuities in a jar decorated in red, black, and white with her name printed on a bow.

In addition to the money in the tip jar, Marylyn Ruzzio found a graduation gift for her son and a check for $100.00.

A note attached to the gift expressed, "Congratulations to Claude Ruzzio, the son of Mr. and Mrs. Ruzzio, from the staff and customers of the Gorham Town Diner."

Chapter 13: "Harassment"

"What is sexual harassment?"

The question surfaced for educators as a result of the United States Senate's hearings in the fall of 1991 on whether President George H. W. Bush's nominee for the Supreme Court of the United States, Clarence Thomas, should be confirmed as a justice on the nation's highest court. During the confirmation process, much of the country heard about the issue of sexual harassment for the first time.

After contentious questioning and debate, with all 100 senators voting, the Senate confirmed Clarence Thomas on a simple majority vote, 52 to 48. As a result of the decision, Justice Thomas occupied a lifetime appointment as a justice on the Supreme Court.

The drama of the confirmation proceedings permeated homes, dinner tables, workplaces, and the media. Moreover, the issue of sexual harassment sparked public policy discussions in schools, in legislative bodies, and in human resources offices.

Ana and I invited our potluck group for a dinner discussion about this topic and how it might affect us in our work with each other and our students. We planned to meet on Friday, October 19, 1991, shortly after the

United States Senate confirmed Clarence Thomas by the close vote. President George H. W. Bush had nominated Clarence Thomas for the Supreme Court on July 1, 1991. The United States Senate confirmed Thomas on October 15, 1991.

Before we congregated, Ana said to me, "Sexual harassment and its implications for teachers and students is yet another matter for teachers to be aware, so discussing the issue with our colleagues is a good idea. In fact, Mark, I believe such a discussion is essential."

I opened the dinner discussion by explaining the confirmation process as accurately as I could: "The president of the United States nominates a person to become a justice on the Supreme Court of the United States. The nomination goes to the United States Senate for "advice and consent." If by a simple majority the Senate approves the nomination, then the nominee takes a seat on the Supreme Court. The appointment is for life unless the justice is impeached and removed from office."

Our potluck group on this evening consisted of Ana and me, Claudia Pace, Megan Straffa, Zack Barber, Cheryl Wattsen, John Browne, April Danniels, Charles Yates, Karla Betts, Jake Spanner, and Lacey Walsh, who joined our group as our newest member.

With the issue of sexual harassment as our topic for the evening, we had more questions than answers.

"What exactly is harassment?" Zack Barber asked. "And, after we delineate that idea, then we need to add the sexual part."

"Yah, and just what are the actions that constitute sexual harassment that can get any of us in trouble?" Jake Spanner followed.

"You guys just don't get it," Megan Straffa asserted.

"What is it that we don't get?"

"Well, Jake, in the work place and in classrooms, you can't create a 'hostile environment,' which is a fundamental concept in defining what sexual harassment is and what harassing does."

On this evening, we did not get very far. The discussion bounced back and forth without resolution. This was a new issue for all of us. We worked on defining terms and limits in relationships. As teachers, we were particularly concerned about how this affected our respective classrooms.

Our dinner group said good night to each other lacking any conclusions. The issue of sexual harassment persisted as the 1990s progressed. We had workshops in school attempting to identify what comprised sexual harassment and how to address the problem when it emerged.

The subject gained traction again in 1998. This time sexual harassment, what it was, and how it manifested itself, directly related to a president of the United States—President William J. Clinton.

After the United States House of Representatives voted on December 19, 1998, to impeach President William J. Clinton, Ana and I again invited our colleagues to a potluck dinner to renew discussions regarding sexual harassment and its implications for our work.

We met on Friday, January 29,1999, for our potluck dinner. I began our session with a series of still unsettled questions:

"What is a hostile environment?"

"How can a hostile environment be identified? Will we know it when we see it? What should teachers do if we are in a hostile environment?"

"What should teachers do if they are accused of creating a hostile environment?"

Megan Straffa added the question, "Is what Derek

Randallston did harassment?"

John Browne asked, "Should Derek have been
removed from the classroom for sitting in a car alone
with a student? As far as we know, just sitting in the
same space with a student was all he was doing. April
Danniels has told us that was the case. Am I right about
that, April?"

"Yes, John," April agreed, "that is correct."

I continued, "What happens when a president
or presidential candidates are accused of sexual
harassment? How about members of the United States
Senate and the United States House of Representatives?
Supreme Court justices? State legislators? Members of
boards of education? City and town council members?
Others?"

As a group, we generated additional questions:
"When we are teaching, what could be examples of
sexual harassment? How do we as teachers deal with
the advertisements depicting scantily clad women
selling products? What should we do in the classroom
when our students get the idea that they should look
like that too? Is it harassment when men and women
use sex to sell products? If not, what is it? Will showing
the advertisements in our classroom open us up to
charges of stimulating the innocent young? Could that
be defined as sexual harassment? Which raises the
question: Where are the boundaries? How do we know
what the confines of behavior are before we get into
trouble?"

Once we got going, the questions flowed: "How about
at sports events when attractive reporters are used
to entice viewers? Are viewers being harassed by the
constant use of sexual innuendos and scantily clad
models? During televised sporting events, how many ads
have women in them as objects rather than as people? Is

harassment all around us? If so, how do we teach about it without being charged with sensationalizing the issue, or getting in trouble ourselves for even broaching the topic?"

"We may be stretching the definition of harassment. Although I am not so sure," Megan said.

"Alright then, how can we as teachers protect ourselves against a charge of sexual harassment?" I asked, "What if a student gets a bad grade and just doesn't like a teacher and makes an accusation? Can a female teacher be accused of harassment? How do we teach without fearing a charge of sexual harassment? How about language in the classroom referring to sexual activity? Is it okay in a historical context, in a sociology class, in a psychology class, or in an English class?"

Charles added, "A number of presidents from President George Washington to the present have been cited for their sexual interest. Is it permissible to talk in class about the indiscretions of public officials? How about important national figures like Alexander Hamilton? President Thomas Jefferson? How about...? The list is a long one.

"What if the charge of harassment, misconduct, or abuse is made, yet we as teachers are innocent and the charge does not hold up, how then do we recover our reputations? Can we and should we talk with our students about sexual harassment in the classroom, in the school, and elsewhere in our society? What can we do in the classroom to protect ourselves from a charge of sexual harassment? What if being careful and doing what we believe is the right thing is not enough?"

Chapter 14: Dr. G.

Dr. Gary Mantino taught for ten years at the state university—long enough and well enough to earn tenure. He published articles in important journals. Other scholars read his articles and cited his books. Yet, like Lacey Walsh, he wanted to teach high school.

When Dr. Mantino applied for a teaching position in the social studies and history department at Bailey T. S. Memorial High School, I was baffled as to why a university professor would want to do such a thing.

I had found Lacey's decision to move from the television industry to high school teaching puzzling. As if her decision did not perplex me enough, we now had someone who wanted to move from college teaching to what was most likely a more difficult task than instructing college students—teaching teenagers in high school.

When I interviewed Gary, I asked him, "Gary, why would you want to move from teaching in college to high school? You will make less money, your classes will most likely be larger, and you will have less prestige—much less.

"Teaching history to high school students will be a different experience than teaching college students, and I believe, much more difficult. So, Gary, why are you here interviewing for this job?" I asked.

"Hmmmm, Mark, I have wondered about that myself," Gary said with a sly smile.

"What have you come up with?"

"First, and most important," Gary explained, "I find high school students in their teen years absolutely fascinating. The one downside, however, is that I will have to wear a tie. In college teaching, there was no such requirement."

"I never thought about that, but you wouldn't be here if you thought donning a tie as too much of an obstacle," I said grinning.

"On the contrary, a tie should be a way to distinguish myself from the students. Of course, I believe I can still wear my 'professor's shoes,' better known as walking shoes. The shoes are without a sheen except from excessive wear. I am assuming they will work at Bailey High."

"Yes, indeed, Gary, if you teach here then you will be wearing the high school teacher's 'uniform,' a tie— yet even the tie is not compulsory, although it used to be when Mitchell Appletone was superintendent," I explained. "The comfortable footwear is your choice. Some of our teachers choose white shoes or even bright orange and even green to signal they are different. Most teachers wear the conventional black, although you might see Karla Betts, an art teacher, and Zack Barber, a social studies teacher, wearing shoes in multiple colors.

"More seriously, Gary, besides the age-level of the students and variable dress, there must be additional reasons why high school teaching appeals to you, especially considering what you will be giving up—the prestige of teaching in college."

"There are, indeed, more substantial reasons. Although, I believe teaching high school students who have their future in front of them is an important reason," Gary said.

"I agree, Gary. What we do is important work."

"To go on then, Mark, I was getting increasingly unhappy as a tenured college professor. The politics of university work frustrated and overwhelmed me. The stakes were usually low, but my stress level could get very high. Higher education politics yield minimal rewards.

"I gradually realized that seemingly endless college politics were becoming an obstacle to my ability to teach well. I value teaching and research equally. However, as I came to understand it, the university valued research more than teaching. Publishing in certain kinds of publications was valued over others. I believe there is a lot of evidence to support my understanding that the primary goal of a university is to produce research in prestigious journals, and I did do some of that. To be facetious for a moment, the students sometimes get in the way of that effort."

Gary continued, "In general, the university and the department I was in were keenly interested in the grants and funds we could receive for research. So, as much as we said we were not all about dollars, we were. And as much as we said we were about teaching, we weren't. Teaching was an afterthought for some of my colleagues. They worked almost as hard to get out of teaching as they did on their research."

"How did they do that?" I asked. "Get out of teaching I mean. Doesn't everyone have to teach a certain number of classes?"

"Mark, there are a variety of ways to teach less and in some cases only a course or two. Depending on the size of the grant or grants you obtain, you get released from teaching some courses. After a while, you are only teaching one or two courses a semester. A professor may then be able to assign a teaching assistant to teach one or more of the courses. If this leaves just one remaining course, and the course is a graduate course, the faculty member may have just a few students enrolled. Thus, the professor won't be 'bothered' by undergraduate students knocking on the door during office hours."

"So, Gary, are you telling me that the system is providing faculty members with time to do research and anything else a tenured professor wants to do? And in that case, completing research is the way to advance at the university?"

"Yes, that is generally how it happens in a 'research-oriented' university," Gary agreed. "If you are not teaching undergraduate courses, you don't have many students because graduate courses usually have low enrollments. Consequently, the faculty member has more time for research which gets you promoted and increases your salary. Thus, the reward cycle is completed."

"How do universities justify this?"

"Well, there is a justification. Depending on your point of view, it makes sense. As I have already said, research is important. New knowledge helps to inform researchers and the public; recognition is bestowed on the university.

"I, on the other hand, put teaching first and research second," Gary declared. "You have to conduct research to teach. So, I did a lot of research. I just did not publish it all. I used it in teaching, but if it wasn't published publicly then it was not recognized as 'real' research or counted as research.

"I used research in class. I used it to teach and,

hopefully, the students learned from my inclusion of research in my classes. Yet, according to the 'academy,' if it was not published in some way beyond the university then it didn't exist in the reward structure even though I used the research in teaching. I considered teaching a way to get my work out into the public—publishing my work orally in class. However, that doesn't get you very far if it is not published beyond the classroom or the university's walls."

"Lacey Walsh, who teaches in our department, moved to high school teaching from the television industry," I said. "She said that commercial television is all about money. I thought colleges and universities were purer."

"They aren't, Mark. They aren't," Gary said, shaking his head. "However, it is a different kind of impurity."

"Tell me more about how things work in the university as you perceive them."

"In the scheme of things, college professors don't make that much money. And to be fair, most professors are dedicated to learning and sharing what they learn. Most share their research in the classroom through teaching. Furthermore, some professors convey their research through academic conferences and publish their work through scholarly journals. So, there are a variety of ways to get one's work out in the public. The problem with the university I was in is that there was one big way. As I mentioned, publishing in refereed journals."

"That sounds like professors are doing their jobs in one way or another."

"They are. A lot of professorial time is spent well and doing good things—thinking, inventing, dialoguing and so forth. However, some professors spend their time politicking," Gary explained. "They spend a lot of time playing politics because the stakes in college, as I said before, are so low. Students, however, argue that the political stakes are high for them and should not to be dismissed as trivial."

"In general, Gary, how would you explain to the general public the system you have been describing to me?"

"The best way to explain how some university faculty members work is as follows: If you do not like teaching, are not very good at it, or you would rather be conducting research, then you find a way to concentrate on research. The fewer students you have then the more time you have to advance your career through publishing your research.

"It all makes sense. The more students a teacher has, the more time teaching requires, and the less time you have for other things. Ergo, the cynics argue that you just keep the enrollments down which is a way to succeed as a university professor. Of course, let me repeat myself, not everyone does this. Some professors teach lots of students and do cutting-edge research that gets published. Over-generalizing what happens at a university can be misleading, but you asked, so I am trying to explain what happens in some cases at the university I taught at."

"Why would students go to a university like that?" I asked.

"At the university where I taught, we use football, basketball, and other games to attract people to become students. We also use the academic rankings that various magazines and publications enumerate. So, if the football and basketball teams don't attract a student, maybe a college's academic ranking will. Academic rankings have little to do with how well students are taught and how well they learn."

"How then, Gary, will parents and students know

how good a university is in meeting its mission?"

"Good question, Mark. I recommend to parents that they ignore the rankings published by the rating agencies. I believe students should decide which college will work for them regardless the 'so-called' rankings," Gary said.

"I understand your analysis, but research and the resulting knowledge are important," I pointed out. "Also, many countries in the rest of the world envy our university system and send their students to universities in the United States."

"Yes, research and the production of knowledge are important. I agree. What I am saying is that it ought not be the only thing or maybe even the primary thing. And, yes, the higher education system in the United States is arguably the best in the world. Many students around the globe aim to attend a prestigious university in the United States. That said, one more addendum to our discussion, I have been talking about research universities.

"Don't get me wrong—even in research institutions, there are some great teachers who are committed to students and teach them well. The problem is that they frequently find that they should have been doing more research and publishing if they want job security, a higher salary, and a promotion.

"And, Mark, there are colleges in this country where professors teach four courses a semester and have 120 or so students. So, as I said, I don't want to over-generalize. The faculty work diligently in the colleges in which they teach large numbers of students. In some cases, faculty members work so hard and are so busy, there is not enough time to go to the bathroom toward the end of the semester. The professors in these institutions have too many students to provide significant individual attention to their students. Students from families who lack financial resources attend these colleges where faculty have less time for them. Insufficient resources and large class loads leave faculty with little time to attend to their students individually.

"The 'so-called' prestigious, well-funded, private universities emphasize teaching and research. They charge high tuition and have the resources to keep classes small. These institutions have full-time faculty teach the classes. The affluent privates provide their faculties with time for research and time for students.

"So, Mark, as I think you can see, the university system in the United States is made up by a variety of institutions and serves diverse populations. However, the faculties may not be diverse, but that is a whole other issue altogether."

"Gary, I get the point," I said, "but I am still having a hard time understanding why you want to teach at Bailey High. You would be giving up tenure. You would end up teaching more courses at Bailey High than you would at a college, and you would have more students. You will make less money. Gary, you must admit, this is hard to comprehend."

"Yup! All of that is true. I would be giving up a lot," Gary said. "I would have more teaching to do, and the secondary school system in this country may not be a whole lot better than working in higher education. Still, I like teaching students and at Bailey High I would get to do that. In fact, I would love to do that. Bring it on. So, Mark, here I am. I am Bailey High's if you want me."

"Gary, I will talk to my colleagues to see what they think," I said, "and I will have to check with the administration. I will let you know if we are able to hire you. If we do—in this high school—students will call you Dr. G."

"I like that. How did that come about?"

"In the late 1960's, there was more informality in the classroom and in school buildings in general. Students using a teacher's first name was considered too informal, and the mister with the last name was too formal. So, the students came up with the idea of calling teachers by using Mr. and Ms. along with the first initial of their first name. It has worked for us and has become a tradition in Bailey High," I explained.

The Gorham school district offered Dr. G. the job.

Chapter 15: MK

I last saw MK a year ago. Ana and I enjoyed picnics with Ricky and Maria Brezos. We had known their children since birth.

On the first day of school in the fall of 1992, I called the roll. Ana and I had not seen MK for a while so when I called the name in my freshman world history class ("Megan Karla Brezos") I was surprised when the Brezos' daughter answered. She was not who I remembered or expected, nor did she reply the way I anticipated. She responded, "From now on, Mr. M., I will only answer to MK."

MK had added some bright red to her hair. I couldn't miss her nor did the spike of red on the top of her head signify, "Miss me." From MK's appearance and attitude, I would not have expected she was the daughter of an educator and a policeman.

In addition to her spiked-hair and color beckoning notice, MK had perfected attitude. Indeed, knowing her conventional, upstanding parents, Megan Karla was not who I imagined. She bounded into her freshman year at Bailey T. S. Memorial High School.

Megan Karla did not turn out the way Ricky and Maria Brezos had planned, or hoped, but MK was MK.

She communicated verbally and non-verbally that she liked it that way.

The Brezos tried to raise their daughter their way. It was the way they thought they should like most parents try to do. MK ignored guidance and rebelled against commands.

Ricky and Maria married in their teens. They brought a baby girl into the world six months later. The last thing they wanted their little girl to do was emulate the mistakes they believed they made in life. As a parent and a teacher, I understood the reality that insisting "my child will not make the mistakes I did" is a recipe for mimicry.

Ana and I realized from our early marriage how difficult it could be for young parents to raise a child. When Joel came along shortly after we got settled in Gorham, Ana and I had to figure out parenting on the go. MK's parents, as with most parents, did the same. Parenting lacks control groups—there is no redo.

In Gorham, it appeared to Ana and me as if Ricky and Maria were doing fine. At least, it looked that way from a distance. Most who befriended the family knew the Brezos as dutiful citizens. Ricky and Maria each had professional jobs and made enough money to provide for their children.

When MK enrolled in elementary school, she excelled in the early grades. Prior to her teen years, she participated in a variety of sports. In the early 1990s, MK entered her teen years. That is when her attitude toward life and school changed. Her parents' patience unraveled.

Ricky Brezos had completed his high school education at night as he said he would. Shortly after high school graduation, he took a job as a security guard. He also worked at the Gorham Town Diner monitoring the counter and waiting on tables.

While working multiple jobs to support his family, he completed his associate degree in law enforcement at the local community college. He interviewed for and started his dream job as a patrolman with the Gorham Police Department. By the time I had MK in my history class, Ricky had been with the police force for ten years. He progressed steadily through the ranks, earning recognition and promotions.

Maria Brezos also had earned her high school diploma. Nancy Cash, Ana's friend at the elementary school they both taught at, obtained a grant for a special education assistant. The grant did not provide enough to pay a fully certified teacher, so Nancy asked Ana, "Do you know someone who would be good working with special education students? We can't pay much, but I would like to find someone good. These kids need and deserve someone who can help them. Any ideas?"

"Yes, Nancy," Ana said. "I do know someone. I recommend Maria Brezos. She has had various jobs taking care of children. I have heard that she does a great job helping children from a variety of backgrounds. She knows what it is like to work hard. Maria has overcome a lot and could help students in special education. I believe she has even taken some courses in the specialization. From my conversations with her, she has a good feel for how hard it is for some people to gain an education."

Maria Brezos began her work as a teacher's aide in September 1988. By then, her daughter, MK, was in fifth grade and MK's younger brother, Kenny, was in the third grade.

When MK matriculated in Bailey High, she had developed into a young, self-assured woman with a mind of her own. In my class in the fall 1992, I made the mistake of assuming what a student would be like without knowing her. I had been teaching for over two decades and should have known better than to assume anything about a young person.

Ana and I had attended various social occasions with the Brezos. Over the years, we got to know both MK and Kenny. MK surfaced in Bailey High as a mischievous and fun-to-be-with teen.

MK needed time to grow and find herself. As she and her younger brother, Kenny, matured, the older sister took care of her sibling. It was clear the Brezos' family love was strong and freely given.

As a loving and responsible husband and father, Ricky Brezos had evolved from a troubled teenager into a conventional, law and order policeman and parent. When Ricky tried to discipline his eldest offspring, MK resisted.

Maria, as a teaching assistant, understood more about child development and the process of growing than Ricky. As a result, she gave MK and her brother more latitude. When MK asked for something, Ricky yielded a hasty "no." Maria, on the other hand, usually helped MK resolve the test of wills between father and daughter. Maria responded to MK's requests with a "maybe, let's see what your father thinks and then we will talk about it as a family."

In my classes, MK thought critically about the subject matter. She energetically defended herself in debates. When issues of social justice developed, MK pursued fairness.

The Brezos asked us to dinner one evening. One topic led the agenda—MK. Ana and I were glad to be invited. We were willing to discuss with Ricky and Maria any issues we could be helpful.

Shortly after we arrived at the Brezos', Ricky

identified his concern. "Maria and I do not know what to do with Megan Karla. Do you have any ideas to help us?"

"Ricky, could you give us some examples of MK's behavior that you are talking about?" Ana asked.

"Yes, to start, her hair color really bothers me. Actually, it is that she colored her hair at all that bothers me," Ricky explained. "And other things bother me too. I guess it all started when she colored her hair without asking me."

"She knew you would have said no, Ricky. So, why ask?" Maria pointed out.

"Well, Maria, she should have asked me," Ricky insisted. "You are right. I would have said no, but she should have asked anyway."

"Ricky, that is my point exactly. That is why she didn't ask," Maria said. "She knew what you would have said, and if you had tried to stop her it would not have turned out well."

"Like I said, she should have asked. I also have a long list of other things Megan Karla does that bother me. I know we don't have time to discuss them all. The truth is that it disturbs me to no end that I am a policeman and I can't even control my own kids—colored hair, rebellion, and all. Her brother isn't much better," Ricky lamented.

"RICKY, it may be because the hair upset you at first," Maria argued, "that everything else on your MK list disturbs you. Maybe we ought to just let her be herself and let her decide things for herself. After all, it is her life."

"Maria, I can't stand it. What you just said might be true, but it drives me nuts," Ricky said.

"Ana and Mark, I think Ricky is way too hard on our children and has made judgments about them," Maria explained. "And, Ricky, you don't want to crush our daughter's spirit, do you?" Maria stared at her husband as she spoke.

"I don't know about that, Maria. I just don't want my children to turn out the way I did." Ricky countered.

"I think you may be too hard on yourself and how you turned out," Ana said.

"Ana, explain that to me, please. I was a royal screw-up. Sorry for the language, but I am sure Mr. M. remembers how much I messed up when I was in high school."

"Ricky, I think you have accomplished a lot in your life," I said.

"I don't see it that way. I got married early. I had to struggle to get a high school education. If I had a four-year degree from college, I could have moved up faster in my job," Ricky explained. "As I see it—I am a failure."

"Oh, come on Ricky, you are a respected policeman," Ana argued. "How can you call that being a failure?"

"Okay, Ana—I am a partial failure."

"Well, Ricky, I don't see it that way—you as even a partial failure," Ana declared. "I don't think Mark does either, or anyone else who knows you. You have a good job with a steady income. You provide for your family. You have a lovely wife who is an outstanding educator, and, Ricky, you have two loving children, who, like you, will be fine productive citizens someday. They just have to navigate life for themselves—just like you did."

"I agree with, Ana," I said. "I don't see you as anywhere near being a failure. Besides, each of your children is healthy and appears to be happy. They are just growing up and moving through their teen years. Growing up as a teenager today is not easy. Taking all that into consideration, what is the problem?"

"Mark and Ana," Ricky said solemnly, "I do not want

them to make the mistakes I did."

"Ricky, they have to live their own lives," Ana said.

"Do you mean that even when they are not yet adults, I have to let them make their own decisions?" Ricky asked.

"Yes. I am afraid you do," Ana said. "Of course, except for when their safety is involved."

"What if my kids make mistakes?" Ricky countered. "And what if they make mistakes that can't be made right?"

"Ricky, it is their lives to live. Your children are going to have to find their own way—mistakes and all," Ana pointed out.

"That idea just absolutely frightens me."

"Along with some of the missteps there will be lots of successes too," Ana said.

Ricky sighed. "Oh, my God. I hope so."

"So, Ricky, problem solved. Right?"

"Huh, I am not sure what you mean, Ana," Ricky said.

"Love them as they grow. They will discover their paths in life."

"Oh, I wish I was sure of that."

"Ricky," Ana said, "in life absolutely nothing is a sure thing."

"Geesus," Ricky swore under his breath.

Chapter 16: "Union"

"What possible reason could there be for not wanting a strong union?" Claudia asked. "I don't get it. I can't believe how much we let the school board and the administration push teachers around. We need to organize, unite, and fight for our students. That's what teachers' unions do."

"I am not so sure, Claudia, what do you recommend we do?" Zack countered.

"Zack, let me provide a little background," Claudia said. "When I taught in Appalachia, I was remiss in my failure to strengthen the union in the community in which I taught. I vowed after I left that job, I would not make the same mistake again, and I won't.

"We were talking at a recent potluck about sexual harassment and that charges could be made against teachers. A union could help to defend us and make sure we are treated fairly on that issue and others that matter to us."

Even though, like Zack, she had libertarian tendencies—or maybe because of them—Claudia believed teachers needed a union because management was already united. She argued, "The administration speaks in a single voice. Teachers should also speak in unison through a concise message. We frequently don't speak as one, but I believe we should. We need to be free to teach."

Claudia incorporated some of Megan Straffa's "take no prisoners" assertiveness with an "I don't care what you think" attitude. When Claudia thought she was right it was prudent to move aside if you were in the way.

At a potluck dinner, Claudia again asked the group consisting of Jake Spanner, Karla Betts, John Browne, Zack Barber, Claudia Pace, April Danniels, Lacey Walsh, Megan Straffa, Cheryl Wattsen, Charles Yates, Ana, and me, "Why don't we have a strong union? I don't get it."

Cheryl responded, "What is it that you don't get Claudia about our union? We have a teachers' association. I believe it is functioning."

"Unfortunately, it is functioning. I believe having a union is not necessary and not necessarily a good idea. So, Claudia, if it is not functioning—I am glad it isn't. I recommend we just drop the idea of having a union." Charles said.

"I beg to differ, Charles," Claudia argued. "Our salaries are low. Our benefits are paltry. We don't have rights. We are afraid to push back. That is just part of our problem. We let the administration and the school board push us around. We need to stand up for ourselves and for our students. If we don't stand up for our interests and our students, who will?"

"What you say makes sense to me, Claudia. In the past, I didn't believe we needed a union, but I am beginning to see your point," I said. "We need to protect ourselves and each other. Okay then, what should we do, and what can we do to strengthen our position?"

"Mark, and everyone, let me reiterate what happened

when I was in Appalachia," Claudia explained. "I realize that the towns were no longer called 'company towns' when I was there. However, I think they were de facto company towns. The company got its way and still does; the public gets screwed. Here in Gorham, the town's administration gets its way. In this community, the administrators serve the bidding of the powers that be. We need a strong union as a counter.

"Since I have been here, I have learned that in many ways Gorham is no different than what is known as a company town. Powerful industries and businesses run the show. I realize what I am about to say is a strong comment, but the power dynamics in Gorham and the surrounding communities are interrelated. The corporations have power, and they use that political power to enforce their hegemony. A small group of people calls the shots. These folks are powerful. They tell us what to do, they control the curriculum, and they try to make sure we don't get out of line."

"Claudia, what you are saying is, indeed, a strong statement," I said. "I, for one, have never thought of Gorham and similar towns to be quite that way. Maybe your comments are too extreme. At least, your comments are too strong for me."

"Well, Mark, maybe so, but my experience is that corporations and businesses control the reins of government," Claudia continued. "Their directives regulate the populace. In that sense, it is like what we have in Gorham and where I taught previously in a company town. In the company towns, the company owned and influenced everything, and I mean everything—the store, the mines, the schools—everything. We tried to organize but ran into roadblocks.

"The miners' children were in our schools, so some of them saw first-hand what we were trying to do to help them. Most of the students sympathized with our cause. When asked by their parents or relatives, they reported what they heard in school. Out of context or even in context, students reporting home led to trouble for teachers who questioned the status quo. The students did not want to get us in hot water, but sometimes just mentioning what we had talked about in class generated a note from the administration that we had gone beyond the 'approved' curriculum.

"We tried to protect ourselves, but the bosses in town and the school administrators did not want us to organize. If we had been successful in organizing, workers in other industries might have gotten ideas. The powers that be were generally successful at shutting down attempts to organize.

"Labor laws prevented companies from directly interfering in labor organizing, but there seemed to be ways around the law. Had we organized, we might have been able to fight back. In the absence of a strong union, we got shoved around and pushed out of the way. This was not good for us or our students.

"When I taught in a company town, workers could get in trouble if they were overheard even talking about joining a union. There were management spies everywhere watching for pro-union activities. The spies reported to the owners and the school administrators.

"Eventually, the owners found out what the union advocates had planned. The organizers were undermined, and the leadership neutralized. Teachers and other employees soon discovered that anyone who expressed or hinted at union sympathies saw their positions eliminated."

"Maybe it could happen to us here," Charles said.

"It could, Charles," Megan said. "In fact, because we are not unionized, it is already happening. Remember what happened to Derek Randallston? In the past, the administration forced out anyone who was perceived as a threat to the status quo. I believe that our only protection is to come together and support each other— in a union!"

"If the teachers had been unified, Derek—who, according to everyone I've spoken to, was a good teacher—would have had some rights and a fair hearing," Claudia pointed out. "A strong union may have been able to support him, and our students would have benefitted from having a good teacher."

"So, what do you think we ought to do, Claudia?" Zack asked. "My political philosophy, libertarianism, is against unionizing. However, I, too, am getting tired of management's elbows."

"Zack, I believe we should strengthen our association and turn it into a full-fledged union. Then we come together, fight like hell, protect each other, and advocate for a quality education for each of our students. That is what I believe we should do," Claudia explained.

"I am all for that. I am with you, Claudia," Karla said.

"How do we do that? HOW?" Zack vented his frustration and then went on, "We know the history. President Ronald Reagan's administration broke the Professional Air Traffic Controllers Organization Strike in 1981. Before the year ended, the government decertified the union. Some of its 13,000 members were out of their jobs. As a result, the out of work union members found jobs harder to get.

"Reactionaries loved Reagan's anti-union actions. He had broken the strike. It wasn't the 1920s, but it was reminiscent of strike-breaking. Union families soon realized they did not have a friend in the White House. I am generally not a union-type, although I can see Claudia's point. I can go either way—union or not."

"Everyone, the move toward an all-out union could bring a load of trouble upon us," Cheryl argued. "If we organize a union, the same de-certification action could happen to us. We could all be out of jobs. The government and the elite power structure control the levers of authority.

"Maybe the old cliché, 'you can't fight city hall' is the case in Gorham. We could be black-listed and find it difficult to get jobs as teachers, or as anything for that matter. My lawyer husband, Cliff, said that forming a union could be, to use his words, 'risky business.' I am not sure forming a union is a good idea."

"So, do we just continue this way, and allow our students to miss out on a quality education? Can't we fight back? Can't we fight for the resources to educate our kids?" Jake asked.

"Hey, Charles and Cheryl, why do people get so upset about teachers unionizing but give a pass to some other kinds of public unions? Why?" Claudia asked. "I realize the political climate—if not anti-union—is at the very least not friendly to unions in general, but especially to teachers' unions.

"The real battle is about our students getting a good education. For some reason, taxpayers seem to have a problem with teachers joining together and fighting for their rights. I wonder why that is the case. Teachers have a right to battle for their members. Other employees do too. I believe it is the American way. To use another cliché, it is 'as American as apple pie' to fight for our rights and for the population we serve."

Jake added, "The public has heard from the management. Management and businessmen own and manage the news media. The public hears more of one side of the story than the other. Also, Gorham's school board gets its messages out through their friends in the media. We have to do more to get our side out."

"Members of the public in some communities have been critical of teachers coming together into a union," I said. "However, as some of you have said, 'Management is a union.' They are by nature together and speak in one voice and the result is an effective, unified message. We need to come together too. If someone in management does not toe the company line, then they are out of there. We need to communicate to the public a concise message promoting our positions on education issues. Maybe a union can do that."

"Mark, I agree with what you are saying." Claudia said. "Corporations own the various media and their managers do their bidding. So, the anti-union message is what the American people hear. As a result, the various media—owned by the controllers—get to tell their story. Unions try to tell their side of the story, but often experience little success when spreading messages through the corporate-controlled media. In addition, the union's reason for existence has been belittled, thus marginalizing unionized educators.

"Some newspaper editors place the union's position on page fifteen rather than on the front page where the management position is featured. At least in newspapers the union's position is there if a reader looks for it opposed to television, where the heads of some of the networks tolerate unions in their own companies only because they absolutely must, but seldom prominently feature them on the nightly news."

Claudia Pace as a teacher at Bailey Memorial was in no mood to move again. She hinted now and then that she might return to what she called "home," but not until she had stood up for her colleagues and students in Gorham. Then, as she said, "I will be ready to stand up to power back home," wherever home was to Claudia.

At this juncture, she was ready to battle right here in Gorham, Massachusetts. However, she realized she needed political cover. Claudia was convinced a strong union would protect her and her colleagues.

Cheryl asked, "What should we do, Claudia? You have some experience with unions and were thinking about organizing when you were in Appalachia. As I said before, my lawyerly husband, Cliff, says we should be careful. Not that we shouldn't do anything to defend ourselves and help our students, but that we should be aware of the downside because we are dealing with the power structure."

"I have been checking things out," Claudia explained. "Our so-called association of teachers has a president, secretary, and treasurer. We hardly ever hear from them, and they rarely meet. I recommend the first effort is to increase the association's membership and then convert the association into an active union."

"Although, Claudia, in general I am in favor of what you are talking about, I am reluctant to proceed. Are we sure we want to do this at this time?" I asked. "It would consume a lot of time and energy. We have other things we need to do. And we would be going up against some influential people with a lot of clout."

Half laughing, Claudia said, "I have known you for a while now, Mark. It did not take long for me to discover that, to say the least, you are cautious and push things off into the future if you possibly can."

"I think we all agree that Mark navigates slowly," Cheryl said to our chuckles. "Although, I agree with Mark's temperate stances most of the time."

"I don't see the humor," Charles said. "I think Mark's measured approach is the right one. In fact, I am anti-union. I don't want any group telling me what to do. We are doing fine here in Gorham, and, yes, Mark, if you do go ahead with a union, which I am against, I recommend that you be very careful. Cheryl's advice to watch out is something I support. I don't want anyone committing us to a union until we know all the facts, and even then I am not sure it is a good idea."

"I hear you Charles, but I plan to go to the next teachers' association meeting. I plan to raise some hell. I have been quiet long enough. I realize that I could possibly risk my job if I go up against those in control—but screw it," Claudia said.

"I would like to go with you, Claudia," I agreed. "I haven't been to many of the association's meetings. Although, I am a "dues" paying member of the organization. I hear what Charles is saying. So, I would like to go to the association meeting and offer another side if necessary—not an anti-union message, but a message of caution. The more we talk I am actually becoming in favor of some action, but with my usual note of caution."

"Mark, please do come with me to the association meeting. We need a union that can act for our interests. You and I can raise some hell together. Although, I am not sure you are the hell-raising kind," Claudia said to laughter. "You can slow the train down if you think we are moving too fast and if you see a major downside, but, seriously, we need to go and fight for the kids. I really believe that is what teachers' unions can and should do—fight for the kids."

"I think even Charles is for that," Megan said.

"I am for advocating for the students' best interests," Charles said, "but it needs to be done the right way, and I think a union is the wrong way to go about it. There are other ways to 'fight for the kids' as Claudia puts it."

"I hear you, Charles, and I think everyone hears you," I said. "However, I am ready to go to the association meeting to see what they are up to. So, Claudia, let's go to the next meeting."

"There may be some hope for you yet, Mark."

"Besides teachers at Bailey High, we may be able to get other public service unions to join with us," I said.

"In fact, the teacher, fire, police, service, and other public unions can and do work together for workers' rights and the community we all serve," Jake explained. "We could all serve the citizens of Gorham better if we strengthen ourselves with numbers by coming together with other unions serving the populace."

"I agree with what Jake just said. We can learn from the other well-organized public unions. We have relatives of teachers and former students, like police officer Ricky Brezos, in various public service departments who could help us think through the steps we need to take to defend and expand our interests," I said. "Claudia, you wanted to say something else."

"Yah, I do. Teachers get the short end of a lot of sticks," Claudia said. "We need to go for it. We need to get active and make some noise."

"I am ready to, at least, start. At the next association meeting, I am going with you," I declared. "I don't know about the noise part, but I plan to be there with you, Claudia."

"That is fine with me, Mark. I will be ready and willing to make the noise," Claudia agreed, "but I think—knowing you as I do—you will get into the swing of things eventually. You might even sound off."

Chapter 17: Angela

Arnold Drake joined the social studies and history department in the fall of 1991. Arnold was never happy teaching at Bailey High. For twenty previous years, he had worked the business world. He soon discovered education was not a business, but a process.

After Arnold sold his company at a considerable profit, a friend suggested he try teaching to occupy his time. Arnold obtained "fast-pass" certification to become a teacher. In the early 1990s, teacher-certification programs outside the traditional university education major path began to entice people who thought they might want to become teachers through alternative certification programs. Arnold Drake took the quick route to the classroom.

Arnold soon discovered he was unprepared to teach high school students. From his first day on the job, he found teaching more difficult than he ever could have imagined. He wanted out.

Mr. A. halfheartedly finished the school year. For some reason, he didn't want the fact that he failed to complete a job on his record. Arnold Drake waited for the last school day in June of 1992 to resign.

Angela Tremonte applied for the open position

in the social studies and history department. As an undergraduate, she had majored in history. She then earned a Master of Arts in teaching. Angela was as committed to changing the world as a teacher as Arthur was to leaving the profession.

In her efforts to make a difference, Angela had campaigned for political candidates in a state that held the first in the nation's presidential preference primaries—most recently supporting candidates in the 1992 New Hampshire primary.

In the job interview, Angela explained to me some of what she had learned campaigning for presidential candidates in New Hampshire primaries. "The state has relatively few minorities rendering it different from some other early battleground states in the United States presidential elections. New Hampshire's voting population is considered well-educated and informed about political issues.

"So, Mark, even though the state is small and possessed only four electoral votes in 1992, New Hampshire's out-sized influence in presidential campaigns, with just four electoral votes, derives from the fact it has held a preferential primary since 1916, and has been the influential first in the nation presidential primary since 1952."

"Angela, California has more electoral votes," I said. "Yet, since 1952 New Hampshire's sway upon the eventual Democratic and Republican nominees has been greater than its population warrants. Why would you say that is the case?"

"Yes, indeed, Mark. New Hampshire, being the first, attracts national media attention which accounts for its impact," she said.

"How were you involved in politics?" I asked.

"From the time I was old enough to do so, I campaigned

for Democrats in the New Hampshire primary," Angela explained. "I distributed brochures and flyers to people on their way to vote on election day. My father had served as a city councilman and had been active in politics since he was a teenager. Dad moved from job to job to make enough money to keep our family above water. He liked and still likes the freedom that serial employment provides. That way he has time for his real love—politics. He continues to be addicted to political activity. Since I was in kindergarten, I campaigned for him and for others we both supported. I became addicted to politics. Still am."

"So, you are what we would call a 'political junky.' You are hooked on politics. Is that right?" I asked.

"Yes. I guess you could say that. Although I am just a student of politics now, I want to teach about what I have learned."

"Are you still committed to political action?"

"No, Mark, I am a recovering activist," Angela said. "I still pay close attention, read everything I can about politics which feeds my political addiction, but am no longer active. Instead, I intend to convey what I have absorbed from participating in practical politics. I want to help students learn about active citizenship."

"That all makes sense, Angela," I agreed. "So how did you get interested in teaching?"

"My mother is a teacher. She is the primary breadwinner in my family. As a school teacher, and even with a paltry teacher's salary, my mother has always earned more money than my father ever did. His obsession with politics has cost my family in material terms, but has added to a sense of civil participation. I appreciate that I have had a chance to be involved in politics. Even though I didn't serve in office, I believe active citizenship is essential to our country.

"Instead of earning much of an income, my father taught me about political action. He still spends most of his earned income on his political habit. If you add it all up, a teacher's salary and my father's occasional income-producing jobs, you can see I did not grow up in a wealthy family. However, early in my youth I did learn about politics and the importance of citizen involvement," Angela explained.

"As a teacher for over twenty years, Angela, I can vouch for a teacher's family lacking riches," I joked. "Why do you want to teach?"

"Over the years, watching my mom, has driven me to become a teacher. My mother is so committed to education and teaching. I guess I am following in her footsteps. From an early age, I wanted to become a teacher like her. She has inspired me to help students. So, that is my main motivation for teaching—to be like my mother and do what she has done all her life. She helps young people learn—I want to do that too."

"I can understand the inspiration part," I said. "I have had the good fortune of working with some great teachers here at Bailey High. I have found them to be inspiring. In most cases, I wish I could be as good as they are, but I do the best I can. And, Angela, I am me, and you will have to be who you are—living up to your values, abiding by your ethics, and practicing your philosophy through teaching and learning."

"I agree with what you are saying, Mark. I would just like to be as competent and capable as my mother someday," she said. "She has been a good citizen, lived up to her values, and been a model for young people on how a participant in a republic should behave. I want to do that too, but I will have to do it my way."

"It sounds like you have had an exemplary model. What did you learn while working in politics that might help you teach social studies at Bailey High?"

"First, I learned a lot about myself," she explained. "I don't like to play 'smiling face' games. Even if I wanted to put the face on, I wouldn't be very good at it."

"Explain that for me please," I inquired.

"Well, my job in supporting candidates was to seek votes for the candidates I campaigned for," Angela said. "In the process, I had to be nice to some real sleaze-balls because I was scrubbing for their endorsements. Some of these politicos are the kind of people, Mark, you can't stand, but I still needed their support. They are people who vote, and they can get others to vote for their favored candidate. Therefore, you figuratively caress and publicly genuflect to them. It is nauseating.

"These politicos are not the kind of people I want to spend time with. After a while it gets really sickening. I discovered that I did not want to do that any longer. I watched my mother cheerily go teach her classes. I talked with her and decided that teaching is what I want to do. In addition, my mother did not have trouble sleeping. She worked so hard during the day that when she hit the pillow she was in dreamland. When I was glad-handing for candidates, I tossed and turned. I have decided that I want to sleep soundly like my mother."

"You have had a lot of political experience," I commented. "What is it about politics and government that you would teach your students and us—your faculty colleagues?"

"Most of what I learned through my experiences is how government works. There are some good people who are politicians. They get elected, and, in part because of the 'trophies' they receive, it is difficult to leave the trappings of representing the public once they get into office. People call them 'Representative This,' 'Senator That.' They like the sound of what they are called and the tone in which the 'respect' is communicated, even though the so-called respect is from someone who often wants a job or a political favor of some kind. In a very real sense, the respect is tainted and corrupted.

"I learned that the system we have rewards the politicians through non-monetary perks. The politicians accept the admiration and the symbols that accompany political power. They come to believe that they are wanted because of who they are and not what they are. Unless they are different, these politicians want to get re-elected and collect more adulations. In office, their phone calls are returned. Some elected officials forget why they ran in the first place, and start to make compromises. They enjoy the accessories that go along with the office.

"The political organism entraps the politicians entangling and embedding them in the system. In time, the politicos become the system. Most of them never get out, except when the populace kicks them out, which, in my judgment, is often not enough.

"Incumbency protects these guys because they have access to gobs of campaign money. Once elected, unless the politician is indicted—and even then—re-election is almost guaranteed because of the power of incumbency and its fundraising advantages. If a politician has raised enough money, he can ward off challengers. Woe to an opponent who dares to challenge a well-funded incumbent."

"Angela, you said 'guys.' Were they mostly guys?" I asked.

"Yes, they were," Angela said. "Women worked to get the candidates elected, but men were invariably the candidates. I hope it changes someday—it hasn't yet, but there are signs it might."

"How would you teach all this without also teaching

adults and young people to become cynics?"

"Mark, I do not want my students or anyone else to become cynical," she explained. "There are some political participants who are public servants. The answer is to become informed about our system and then go about electing the best representatives we can."

"What do you believe our students need to be informed about?"

"First, I would have my students discover what is in the Constitution of the United States."

"You used the word discover."

"Yes. I believe that just telling students, or telling anyone for that matter, just does not work," she said. "Students must discover knowledge for themselves. There is a lot in the Constitution that I think students should know. They should know why the First Article is first. As you know, the founders believed that the Legislative branch was the most important, so its duties and obligations are listed first. The Executive branch is identified in the Second Article and the Judicial branch is in the Third Article.

"According to the 39 MEN who signed the Constitution in September of 1787, the legislative branch was supposed to be superior. However, television has increased the power of the executive branch. Today, presidents claim media attention at almost any time. Individual members of congress are less likely to gain national attention. Thus, television's power to provide undivided attention distorts the intent of the founders by giving the executive branch informal power not enumerated in the Constitution, or conceivable by the nation's founders.

"It wasn't intended to be that way, but the power of the presidency has grown as the powers of the various media have increased. Television has magnified the office of the presidency as well as the voice and the image of the president. As I mentioned, the intent of the nation's founders was that the legislative branch should be the most powerful. Television has provided the executive branch—the presidency—with the power to affect events the founders of this country did not intend or could have imagined. In effect, the First Article— the legislative branch—has become the second, and the second article—the executive branch—has become the first, Not literally, but in effect."

"Angela, the actuality and the intent in the Constitution's development raises an important question," I said. "Do you think we should help students learn the facts of history and contemporary society, or should we be advocating what we believe to be true?"

"Actually," Angela said, "both."

"I am not sure about that, Angela. I am uncomfortable with the idea that we should advocate. I don't think we should tell students what they 'should' believe or even what they should do. In my judgment, we, as educators, are obligated to stick to teaching history and the principles of government. That is our job. Then we should let students make up their own minds over what should be and what they should do as a result of the information they gain."

"I actually agree with you, Mark. Let me make sure we understand each other. I don't think there is any problem discussing with students possible options as long as they make up their own minds on what should be. I just don't like the idea of choking off any avenue of thought for students."

"I think we agree on students thinking for themselves, but you have to admit there is a fine line in what you are saying."

"Sure, I do, Mark. A lot of teaching is fine-lining.

168

That is part of the art of teaching and what makes the profession so appealing to me."

"Angela, that makes sense."

"I am glad it does," Angela said with a laugh.

"On another topic, obviously related to what you would do as a teacher, what did you learn while working in the 1992 presidential primaries that you believe our students should know?"

"Mark, that is an easy one for me," Angela commented. "I learned that in many cases perception is more important than reality. Televised politics is a classic case of bait and switch; it is the image over the narrative.

"Furthermore, to get on television, a candidate needs money—lots of it—either one's own or through soliciting resources from others to fund campaigns. The donors of the money often want something in return. Some donors want what we would consider good things like improved government—their definition. Some other contributors want nothing in return. They just want to support a candidate they believe in.

"Then there are the plutocrats who back a candidate financially and make it as clear as they can without violating election rules that they want something in exchange for contributions.

"For candidates it is a Faustian bargain; it comes down to the necessity of having the money. Without much money, it is difficult to buy time on television, and if you don't get on television then you have little chance of getting elected.

"If you do get elected because of the money you solicited, you generally owe something to those who helped you get elected. It does not have to be 'quid pro quo,' but it is close. This whole system irritates me. I want to teach about it. Then maybe our students as future citizens can improve the way we do things in this country. I am assuming they will want to change the system in which raising dollars is what political candidates spend most of their time on."

"Lacey Walsh has said in a previous workshop that when she was reporting on campaigns in the television industry that 'getting elected is about three factors: money, money, and more money,'" I said. "Is that how you see it?"

"From my experience—yes. I believe Lacey's analysis is on the mark. Once again this raises the important questions: Do we teach what is or what we believe should be? Do we teach that we have a plutocracy and not a democracy? Or, do we teach that the American system is fine the way it is and that it is our fault if we don't get out to vote for candidates selected by the plutocracy? Indeed, we often have no real choice; ergo, which well-funded candidate who has been selected by the wealthy campaign funders are we going to choose?"

"Hmmm, Angela, I believe these issues you raise are important. You have a clear point of view that our government is run by a small group of people with money."

"Yes, I do," she agreed. "I think the evidence is irrefutable."

"There are some on the faculty who would dispute what you are saying," I pointed out. "We will have to have that discussion. It raises the question of whether the United States is a democracy, a republic, or a plutocracy.

"Our faculty also needs to discuss whether we should be teaching the 'what is?' Or, should we teach about what should be? We have a lot of 'shoulds' don't we?"

"Yes, we do, Mark," Angela said. "Yes, we do. I look forward to the discussions with faculty, students, and anyone else who wants to discuss these issues."

"What if, Angela, the public accuses us of advocating certain positions?" I asked. "What if we are accused of politicizing the classroom?"

"If we are teaching accurately and truthfully, then so be it, Mark," Angela declared, "so be it."

"Isn't truth relative?"

"Sorry, Mark, it isn't"

"Ms. A.," I said, "you sound a lot like Megan Straffa."

"I look forward to meeting her and teaching with her. The question is, Mark, can Bailey High handle both of us on one faculty?"

Chapter 18: "Shaming"

"Ana, Bailey High students are aware that what they look like matters to other people," I explained. "As young people in their teen years, they all too frequently believe that how they look defines who they are as a person. The concern with appearance is constant. For some teens, it can be life-affecting, life-shaping, and, what is worse, life-warping."

"Ouch, Mark—affecting, shaping, warping—this is scary stuff," Ana agreed. "If it is impacting high school students, then it is probably affecting my students at Gorham Center Elementary school."

"Yes, it is most likely affecting younger students like the ones you and April Danniels teach," I said, nodding. "And yes, it is frightening. Certain people in a young person's life—parents, relatives, significant others—judge their appearance and behavior. The influencers have the power to affect how these young people perceive themselves. The constant judgments affect our youth.

"For example, in American society 'thin' is in. Ana, you and I and our children are not what most people in our society would define as thin. The definition of thin is evasive because it is a judgment call. Our society's preoccupation with weight affects virtually every facet of our public persona. Movies and television convey to all of us what we should look like. The desired 'look' is portrayed through the media telling all of us as consumers what we should look like, and what we should buy to look the way the prevailing culture says we should."

"Mark, I believe my elementary school students have bought into this," Ana commented. "Even at an early age they are overly concerned with how they look. They are preoccupied with fitting into some ill-defined image of what they should look like, and, as a result, what they should be like too."

"Similar to your experiences with elementary school students, Ana, my experience with high school students tells me that teenagers can't ignore the pervasive messages about who they should be and how they should look," I agreed. "The consumer ethos has swallowed our young, and the message sent to all of us contains the idyllic body-image. The advertisers market products to teenage consumers to make them 'new and improved.' According to the commercialized ethos, our children are never perfect enough. These messages are repeated over and over until our kids are saturated with and indoctrinated through the image-laden consumer culture.

"After being flooded with commercial messages, teens frequently adopt the advertised-rendering of who they ought to be. Consequently, young people forsake themselves and evolve into someone else's characterization of who they should be. Our students abandon their very being. They then have trouble finding out who they are because they are spending time trying to find out who they are supposed to be— not who they are. This elusive search leads to all kinds of problems—anxiety, identity issues, and a lack of self-confidence."

"Mark, I hope you are wrong about this," Ana said.

"I would feel better if I were," I agreed, "but the way I see it advertisements sell *the look* to the unwary. Schools, relatives, and significant others proceed to reinforce the messages that American society and culture sends—a definition of what beauty is. The notion is then used to sell products.

"For those who don't fit the conventional and preferred image, the stress of being the other can be humiliating emotionally and physically. That includes a lot of us."

"Unfortunately, Mark, I think what you are saying has happened to our Suzie," Ana explained. "Because of all this shaming, she feels awful about who she is and what she looks like. The two have been made to go together. The consumer culture convinces our young that what they look like is who they are."

"As a high school teacher, I have seen the body-shaming take its toll on my students. Intentional or not, our students are shamed. Adults sometimes try to intervene between the shamer and the shamed, often to no avail. We are told we should have a new improved body, be a different person—not the one we are—but someone else's image of who we should be. If we are not careful, we are in danger of sacrificing who we are for someone else's version of who we should be. The phenomenon can result in disastrous consequences."

"Mark, I have suffered some of the messages' effects because I have been told that I weigh a lot for my height," Ana said. "It bothers me to hear that. The goal of appearing the way others think I should is almost impossible to achieve—perfect weight, spotless skin, muscle definition, and a host of other so-called, societally prescribed, desired physical attributes. I am told in so many ways that I am fat. Sometimes it really gets to me. I am an adult—imagine what it does to our Joel, Suzie, and their friends."

"You are beautiful to me the way you are."

"You say that all the time, but I have trouble believing I am beautiful when the relentless images I receive communicate that I am not. As a culture, we inflict pain on ourselves when trying to be perfect. Perfect is perfect—not within our grasp—unattainable by mere humans. The wrinkles and blemishes come and don't go away even when we spend all kinds of money to make them go away. I so wish that I could accept who I am and what I look like. I know you say I am beautiful, but at times I have trouble convincing myself it is true. And I am supposed to be an adult. Looking perfect is not attainable by me, our children, and other people.

"And, Mark, I fear, too, that it is worse for our kids and students today," Ana explained. "Our society says the cult of beauty is changing, but we still seek the indefinable state of perfection. For teenagers, the pressure to fit into the beauty-at-all-costs culture is of prime importance. Acceptance by one's peers is important for adults, but essential for teens. Joel and Suzie, as well as our students, are right in the center of it.

"Who are these body-shamers? And who do they think they are to make others feel less than worthy? I will tell you who they are. They are television personalities, relatives, and so-called friends. Their judgments have a major impact on teenagers and young children. These elementary, middle, and high schoolers are just trying to grow up and feel good about themselves. This relentless critiquing is not fair to anyone."

"Ana. I get it. Then what should we as parents and educators do?" I asked.

"I don't know what to do," she admitted, "but I do know it is not healthy for anyone to be shamed."

Chapter 19: "Goals 2000"

During a professional development day on March 31, 1994, my colleagues and I discussed over lunch the topics raised in morning seminars. The sessions held before noon focused on new federal legislation and how recently passed education laws could shape our work as educators.

At lunch, we deliberated on the more controversial issues in the legislation and the impact on our faculty and the students we teach. Megan Straffa asked, "What are they coming up with now?

"The federal government has no business telling us how to educate. First, there was 'A Nation at Risk,' signed by President Ronald Reagan in the early 1980s. Now, President Bill Clinton signed legislation designed to be fulfilled in just six years, 'National Goals 2000.' It is a different name for the same old thing. Why don't the Feds let us teach, and get out of the way? We know our kids. They don't."

"I agree with the sentiment in your comment, Megan. Yah, why does the federal government keep telling us what to do?" Zack asked rhetorically. "As a Libertarian, I wish they would leave us alone, so we could do our work."

"I am surprised—actually I am not—because you liberals frequently plunge into hypocrisy," Charles said. "I thought you favored having the federal government intrude into our lives—education being no exception."

"In 1865, we needed a Fourteenth Amendment to the Constitution of the United States, so we would eventually desegregate. Otherwise, I believe our educational system would still be segregated," Jake pointed out. "The federal government needs to insure equality for everyone. 'Goals 2000' is an example of the federal government stepping in to equalize things. Megan, you as a liberal should support such efforts."

"Jake, I don't like to be labeled," Megan said. "I also don't like to be told what I should support."

"I get your point," Jake agreed. "I am not telling you what to do, Megan. Go on. What else would you like to say?"

"I try to use my head and not just go along with what liberals, conservatives, or anyone else wants," Megan explained. "In the case of education, those of us who are in the classroom are the ones who should make decisions on what is best for our students. I think that is a liberal position, and—by the way—it is also a conservative position. The politicians should let us teach and get out of the way, especially if they don't know what they are talking about, and it's clear they don't."

"Jake, I am with Megan on this one," Claudia asserted. "The federal government gets involved in education policy because they want our students to be able to compete with countries throughout the world. We are becoming a cog in the machine of crony-capitalism."

"Claudia, sorry, but you are usually with Megan when you and she are bashing capitalism," Charles said.

"Maybe so, Charles, but let me continue. Why not educate the whole person rather than fitting educated 'products' into the economic engine?" Claudia asked. "We dehumanize our classrooms by treating students as products."

"I agree with Claudia on that," Karla announced.

"Furthermore, the politicos always blame the schools and us as teachers for any perceived failures. Most of the politicians have never taught a day in their lives and wouldn't know what to do if they tried to teach," Megan said. "Yet, they are telling us what to do. It is absurd. We are constantly jerked back and forth depending on the whims of both elected politicians and political appointees."

"In general, I agree with you, Megan," Cheryl said. "However, as I have said before, I am not completely against standardized testing because there is some knowledge that can be measured.

"On the other hand, there are some things I don't believe can be measured. The politicians are looking for an easy way to hold educators accountable. They are going to use tests to do that. If you can't count it, according to the Feds, it doesn't exist. However, you can't make it about numbers when it comes to creative writing which is part of what I teach. Creative writing is not measurable. By its very nature, creativity is sensed, felt, and cannot be quantified. I believe Karla agrees with me. I see her nodding in agreement."

"Yes, I agree, Cheryl," Karla said. "As an art teacher, I can testify that creativity defies scientific measurement. As you have said about writing, art is the same thing as with any creative act—it cannot be put into data charts and schemata. It either is creative, or it isn't. Also, what you said in the past about creative writing, art is by its definition innovative and imaginative. The irrelevant data points accountability advocates use to measure learning have nothing to do with what actually happens in classrooms."

"So, what does 'National Goals 2000' mean for what we do in the classroom?" I asked.

"It will have, hopefully, little impact," Megan said. "It is mostly detached from what we do in our classes. We should ignore the number-crunchers as much as we can. We ought to keep doing what we think is right for the students. Screw the politicians and their bean-counters."

"Ah, Megan, we finally agree on something. Bingo!" Charles said.

"Yikes, I must be wrong if Charles agrees with me," Megan said with a laugh.

"No, Megan, you are right about this one," Charles agreed. "The Feds want to control what we teach, how we teach, and how we measure what we teach. They do this even if they don't have a clue what goes on in our classrooms. Few, if any of them, have been teachers. So, I agree with you—people who have not been teachers shouldn't be telling those of us who are what to do."

"I, too, agree with Charles and Megan on this one," John Browne said. "I know I am being sarcastic when I say, 'All we need is more standardized tests. That's all we need in the future—more time preparing students for the tests, giving the tests, and proctoring the tests.' We are doing this while we are losing important teaching time. Taking all these tests bores our students. In fact, preparing students for the tests bores us too. I wonder if the private school kids are required to take these tests. Of course, I am being facetious when I say I 'wonder.' I know that the private school parents have been able to buy their kids a different kind of education—sans the standardization of tests. If the privates do not have to take the same irrelevant, biased, and tedious tests, they have an advantage. I wonder where the politicians send their children to school. I think I can guess. I saw it when I was a student. Unfortunately, not much has changed. The rich get richer as the lower-income students take tests to justify their existence and the testing industry's profitable survival."

We left our luncheon discussion sensing each other's frustration. Once again, politicians who knew little about what we did in the classroom were telling us what to do through the "Goals 2000" legislation. They did not know our students but decided what was good for them. The politicos used the national educational bureaucracy to threaten educators with loss of funding if we did not obey.

Pundits called William Jefferson Clinton, when he was governor of Arkansas, "an education governor." As governor, Clinton lobbied for a set of national goals for education. They were to be in place by the year 2000. Like most politicians, Clinton had never taught in public schools, kindergarten through high school. Except for being a student himself, he had little knowledge of what goes on in the nation's classrooms day in and day out. In Arkansas, Hillary Rodham Clinton, the governor's wife, advocated education reform although she too never taught in the public schools. Politicians meant well, but that was not enough.

In November 1992, Arkansas' governor became President William Jefferson Clinton. Two years later he signed into law "Goals 2000 Educate America Act." The purpose of the legislation was to produce American students who were more competitive in the world's economic marketplace. The legislation provided more funds for pre-kindergarten and adult education. The adult education provisions emphasized preparing people for work—the "school to work" concept. Hillary Clinton, the president's wife, lobbied to get the legislation passed.

As I wrote to our potluck group prior to our getting together for dinner, "Hillary Clinton, as with her husband, lacks experience teaching in elementary, middle, and high schools. I believe the Clintons are trying to do the right thing, but they would be more on the mark if they had been kindergarten through high school teachers for a couple of years during their careers. If they had been classroom teachers, they would know more of what they are talking about and their resulting proposals would be more effective. I look forward to our discussion about 'Goals 2000' and its implications for our work."

During a Friday potluck we held after the professional day, Cheryl Wattsen and John Browne reported on another recent conference where the legislation's implications were explained. After we settled, Cheryl said, "I want to provide some background on what we learned at one of our recent seminars. The Congress of the United States passed the 'National Goals 2000' legislation, and President Clinton signed it. The idea is that by the year 2000, each state will reach a set of education goals mandated by the federal government.

"Therefore, if a student goes to school in Arkansas and transfers to Massachusetts, the student would have approximately the same conceptual development and skill sets—a worthy goal, indeed. However, the legislation assumes students in Arkansas start from the same economic background and educational advantage as students in other states.

"However, if the assumption of equality of educational opportunity in the various states is wrong, students from dissimilar backgrounds will yield different results. In some states, students with disparate economic and educational backgrounds might not do as well on the standardized examinations. Also, students from some states go to schools inadequately funded when compared to other states.

"Consequently, students moving from state to state would be expected to meet standards they might not be prepared for. Some of the students conceivably could become discouraged, not do well on the standardized exams, and eventually drop out of school. This is not the result we as educators want for our students."

"Thank you, Cheryl, for summarizing things," I said. "What you said leads to the obvious question: Should we have a set of national goals? John also attended the conference. John, I believe you have something you would like to add to what Cheryl said."

"Yes, Mark, I do," John agreed. "Following the reasoning of 'A Nation at Risk'—which I believe to be a faulty report—the United States is behind other nations and needs to be competitive with the rest of the world economically. Thus, it has been presumed that the public schools are failing and need reform. I believe that is an unwarranted conclusion.

"Consequently, due to 'National Goals 2000,' we will most likely hear a call for more standardized exams in the future. In my judgment, this is a bad idea based on flawed conclusions emanating from biased reports," John said.

"Megan, you had a question you asked at our luncheon," I said. "I believe it was something like, 'Why don't the Feds let us teach?' Isn't that what you were asking?"

"Yes, Mark, that was the essence of it," Megan said, nodding. "We know our students and they do not so why don't the Feds let us do our job, so we can teach the students. The bureaucrats don't know anything about our students. They are asking us to do something that won't necessarily work with our school population."

"Well, the Feds, including the members of Congress and the president himself, have zero experience teaching public school kids," Jake added. "They think they know what we should do with our students. Many of them send their own children to private schools where their children do not have to take the same standardized exams as public school students which raises the question—why not? If it is good enough for our students, why don't they require the standardization of their children? I think I know the answer, so my question is rhetorical."

"Jake, you said you think you know the answer," I said. "What do you believe the answer is?"

"I believe the rulers' kids have a private experience just for them, and the public school children have quite another school experience which is not meant to be as good as the privates," Jake explained, "because private school parents are paying a lot for their children to get the educational upper hand. That pisses me off."

"Jake, you said, 'not meant to be as good'—what did you mean by that?" I asked.

"Well, if the public school students could compete with private school students for seats in prestigious colleges and could qualify for good jobs after graduation, then the wealthy parents of private school children wouldn't like it—would they? So, even though I don't think it is necessarily intended and I certainly do not believe it is a conspiracy, the private school students have a different experience—one especially for them—which is the definition of private, and, I would add, privileged."

"Jake and everyone, the private school parents wouldn't like it if they lost their advantages. However, they have the power to keep things as they are. They are in control politically," Megan said.

"It sounds like eugenics all over again," I commented. "Even though those in control would say it is not racist,

184

the divisions are apparent to anyone who cares to look. It continues to be a stacked deck against minorities and low-income kids. There are still some pre-ordained winners and the rest pick up the pieces. Very little seems to be changing and 'Goals 2000' won't make things better."

"Yes, Mark, I believe you are right about that," Megan agreed. "Once again, I must say you have come a long way on the issue of inequity from where you were when I first got to know you."

"I guess, Megan, that is a compliment."

'Mark, you can take it as one."

"I think I will. Although, we keep coming up in our discussions with these seemingly intractable problems. As we end our potluck for the night, what should we do about the problem of inequity? I believe 'Goals 2000' will do little to reduce inequity in education, so how do we improve things?"

"I don't know Mark," Megan admitted. "I don't know. Do we just keep talking about the issue?"

"Megan, that is better than not talking about the issue. At least talking about it is doing something," I said.

"Is that enough for you, John Browne?" Megan asked. "Is that enough? If we just keep talking, nothing changes. We need an action plan of some kind, don't we?"

"I am listening," John said.

Chapter 20: "Guilty"

"The power of the Internet is growing day by day. I am not sure it is a good thing. In fact, I am pretty sure it harms as much as it helps," I said as we began a Friday potluck dinner discussion in the spring of 1996.

"Oh, Mark, you are known for being sort of a conservative guy. You aren't also a Luddite who dreads new technologies are you?" Jake asked.

"I get your point, Jake. But, no, I am not being anti-technology. What bothers me is that people are anonymously accusing others of indiscretions. Craven critics use the technology as a shield rather than saying something directly to someone," I explained. "As a result of the 'it is out there' nature of the virtual world, the person receiving the accusation or insult is deemed guilty—sans evidence and without a trial. Unfortunately, there is nothing we can do about it. An unseen, ethereal jury tries and convicts the 'accused' in absentia. The defendant is deprived of a chance to face the plaintiff. Answering the unseen dignifies the allegation."

"Mark, can I add something?" Cheryl asked.

"Sure, Cheryl, please do."

"Mark, because the medium is generally nameless

and faceless, people can say whatever they want. If a teacher is charged with prohibited activity in class, even if the activity never took place or is edited to make it look as if it did, it could be communicated everywhere in a short period of time.

"In the classroom, a recording of one word out of place or a devil's advocate argument that is misinterpreted can lead to a call from an administrator, or a citizen contacts a school board member or a selectman, who then contacts a school official, gets the teacher in trouble, and the 'alleged' action sanctioned—and I emphasize alleged.

"The school board and its staff scrutinize teachers for doing anything out of the conventional or outside the curriculum. Sometimes the disapproval is implicit and leads to teachers pre-censoring what they do or say. If you pre-censor yourself, then you won't present or discuss some content in class because it might be considered too polemical and could get you in trouble. The students miss out when we are afraid to teach about controversial topics in class. I believe we have to address controversy and do so courageously," Cheryl declared.

"Have any of us at this potluck had an experience with something you have said or done, or something others have said that put you in a negative light, only to see the information planted on the Internet later?" I asked.

"YES," Cheryl said quickly. "There are websites with evaluations of my teaching that anyone can get access to. It is very upsetting."

"If you don't mind, would you be willing to identify some of the comments made about you and your teaching?" I asked.

"Well, in at least one case, the evaluation of my

teaching was awful and harmful for me. The student, at least I assume it was a student, proceeded to disparage me and my teaching. It was a terrible evaluation with hurtful comments about me personally, what I look like, and my teaching. I felt like a complete failure. Some words were particularly cruel to me. I would rather not say the words. Just thinking about them sends shivers down my spine.

"Reflecting about the personal critiques brings back the feeling of despair on my part. As I said, I would rather not give specifics because some of it was particularly profane and repeating what was said about me and my teaching makes me sick to my stomach," Cheryl explained.

"It is difficult for me to comprehend that someone would say something negative about your appearance, personality, or teaching. As a former student of yours, it is impossible for me to believe that disparaging things could be said about you," April Danniels asserted.

"Thank you, April, for what you have said. Coming from a former student, I appreciate what you have said in the past and this time. Your comments give me confidence and the will to go on, but I am having trouble getting over being publicly vilified."

"Anytime you need me, Ms. C., I will be there for you. Your teaching and support helped me at a critical time."

"Thank you for what you have said, April," Cheryl said. "However, the pillorying has damaged me in a variety of ways. I try to avoid re-reading the indictments, but I admit I periodically go back to read the words. I discover once more that they were, unfortunately, not part of a bad dream. The venom has stayed with me for a long time and is still stinging me."

"I would like to add, Cheryl, that everything I have heard in meetings at Bailey High," I said, "and the remarks I have heard in the superintendent's office about you as a teacher and as a person have been positive."

"Thanks for saying that, Mark. I appreciate it. But that bad evaluation on the Internet just destroyed my confidence as a teacher and person. I have yet to recover."

"Cheryl, do you believe it was a former student or someone else who has a grudge?" I asked.

"I do not know and don't want to find out," Cheryl admitted. "But why would someone write such poison if it wasn't a student who had been in one of my classes?"

"No idea." I said. "Have you been able to get your confidence back? And, if you have gotten it back, how did you do it?"

"Well, Mark, I don't have a success story to tell you," Cheryl said. "The online evaluation devastated me and deflated my ego. I have been trying to recoup. However, the recovery process has been slow and painful. My confidence is not back yet—not even close.

"There is more. Because of my name being out there in the virtual world, I have been receiving phone calls and emails about some things I did say and some I allegedly said in class. Some of the messages I have received border on threatening—some I perceive as actual threats."

"Ouch!" Megan exclaimed.

"Yes, some of the warnings are frightening. Some of the more serious comments completely distort what happened in class. Alarming remarks have been made about what could happen to my face and body."

"From what you are saying, Cheryl," I said, "teaching is getting dangerous."

"At least, in my case, it appears to be," she agreed.

"You have lots of defenders. Believe me," I tried

to assure Cheryl. "Have you alerted the authorities regarding the threats?"

"No, I have not. However, I have told my husband, Cliff. He has talked to other lawyers in his office and they are deciding what to do next. Cliff told me to keep copies of everything."

"Regarding having our support, yes, you most certainly do. I am sure I speak for others in this room. We know you are a great teacher," Claudia said with conviction, "and Cheryl, we didn't know how much this had been bothering you. Sorry about that, but I for one did not know. Is there anything we can do?"

"I believe I speak for the group in saying you have our support," I agreed.

"Thanks, Mark and everyone," Cheryl said. "The encouragement you have given me helps me go on. Your support is what is most important to me now."

"Anyone else have any other examples of 'you are guilty' in the virtual world?" I asked.

"Yah. You can imagine what kinds of comments I have received over the years," Megan said, "and now through the Internet, I am critiqued all the time. Some of the comments are downright mean, but I try to not let them get to me. I just keep on going. I just try to teach students how to think critically about things. That isn't always easy or popular. As you all know, it takes guts to teach, and, Cheryl, you have what it takes. So—forward."

"Well, as you all have said, the Internet was not as widespread or in as many homes as it is today, but imagine if what happened to Derek Randallston was sent around the web. He may never have been able to get a job of any kind anywhere," Zack commented. "Potential employers could type in his name and find out what happened to him in Gorham. Derek had not been convicted of anything, and as April Danniels , alias Lydia Smith, has said in one of our potlucks, nothing was going on anyway. If something is blasted onto the Internet, then the charge becomes 'a fact' and the accused becomes a persona non grata EVERYWHERE."

"Besides the comments that are made about us as teachers and as people, the other thing that is happening is that teenagers and even pre-teens are sending pictures out on the Internet that they shouldn't be sending to anyone much less into cyber-space where anyone can get hold of them," Megan explained. "So, it is more than just teachers who potentially are publicly shamed, and with kids it is particularly detrimental. They are not ready for the disparagement at their age. We all remember the bullying of Crissy, and how that circulated around the school, even though we, as teachers, did not figure out what was happening until later—in fact, until it was too late. This whole 'guilt by cyber' syndrome and virtual bullying will only get worse unless we do something. But, hey everyone, what should we do?"

"Well, first, even in the early grades I think we need to teach about the impact of the Internet. I mean we should help students become aware of the harm that hurtful comments can inflict on those on the receiving end," April said. "I think we have to start as soon as children begin school. We must teach respect, and the importance of taking great care in what we say about people when others can read what we write. Ana and I have talked about this."

"Yes, we have. I agree completely with April on this," Ana said.

"How then, April and Ana, would you teach that in elementary school and what should we be doing in Bailey High?" I asked.

"Both on the personal level and in understanding what is happening in our society," April explained, "we have to help learners think through what they are reading on the Internet about themselves and others.

"First, we have to help students get the whole story about themselves and others. Just because one or even several people say something does not make it so. Therefore, we need to watch out we don't arrive at conclusions based upon tainted and incomplete evidence.

"In assessing public events, people see things through their own lens. In critiquing an event, we need multiple witnesses before we have a chance to arrive at conclusions about what happened. Even then, there may be more to the story and the facts may be presented out of context. Then, too, if it is an allegation of criminality, there needs to be a trial and cross-examination. On the Internet, there is generally little evidence presented or any cross-examination.

"Of course, most of the comments on the Internet are not accusations of criminality—just harmful—but that is quite enough to convict you in the court of public opinion. We need to help students think critically in this increasingly multi-faceted world."

"I agree, April," Jake said. "This is an important task that we as teachers need to undertake. We need to help our students think critically about the hyped-cyber-world they are in and will be throughout adulthood."

"How do we do that, Jake?" I asked. "How do we help students protect themselves from the salacious? This whole thing is new and difficult to get our minds around."

"I don't know what to do. I simply do not know, but we need to figure out how to help students learn how to live in the world they are in and prepare for the future,"

Jake admitted. "The future will probably be even more complex and complicated than living in today's world."

"In addition, everyone, as teachers we need to teach about the technological changes that we, our students and our society, will all be experiencing in the next few years. It will have both positive and negative effects," I said as we concluded our potluck dinner discussion for the night.

As our colleagues departed for the evening, Ana asked, "After this evening, Mark, now what?"

Chapter 21: "Club"

"Hey Megan, we have started a book club. Would you like to join?"

"Cheryl, are you sure you want someone like me in it?" Megan asked. "I realize I am not the most agreeable or affable person in the world. Also, I need to know more about it."

"I would like to have you join with us for precisely the reason that your unique perspective enlivens every group you are in," Cheryl explained. "I don't find you disagreeable. I believe you just see things in a different way. Any group that wants to learn and read interesting books needs different views, and we want to learn and enjoy what we are reading. I think your various points of view would be refreshing to a group delving into important and sometimes controversial books.

"Especially in a book club like the one I am proposing, Megan, you would emit intellectual sparks provoking us to contemplate issues we usually don't think about. You see the world in unique patterns which gets any group you are in to see things in novel ways. You stoke fiery discussions. We want that to happen."

"Cheryl, I am not sure if what you are saying about me is good or bad."

"My comments are meant as a compliment."

"Oh. Thanks, I think," Megan said. "I agree that atypical and out of the mainstream perspectives strengthen any group. However, not everyone finds me fun to be around because of my serious and contentious nature, but I must be myself. I realize my opinions have an edge to them. I do everything I can to zap obliviousness before it gets into every day parlance."

"Yup, Megan, you sure do. You have a reputation for candor," Cheryl agreed. "I for one value your frankness."

"Hmmm. Okay, Cheryl, tell me more about the book club and my possible involvement. I am listening."

"You have illustrated by what you have taught in your classes that you assign some challenging literature. I understand from some of your students that you are a fellow 'Janite,' and a thoughtful one."

"I am, indeed, a Janite," Megan declared. "Jane Austen was way ahead of her time. *Pride and Prejudice*, *Sense and Sensibility*, *Mansfield Park*, and *Emma* are among my favorite books. She wrote all of them before she died at 41 years—way too young for such a significant voice. Jane Austen's writing has spurred my mind and heart and continues to do so. As Austen has roused my thinking, I try to spark thought among my students in the classroom."

"Megan, I was a bit surprised to find this out. I hadn't realized that you were a Janite until the students told me, and a social studies teacher nonetheless."

"I am glad you found out," Megan said. "I am a closet Janite. I don't tell many people. However, you are an English teacher. I am not surprised you are one. I am proud to be one."

"Not for that reason, although being a Janite would be reason enough—but for other reasons we would love to have you in our group," Cheryl said. "We have five other possible club members. Two are members of the community and three others are teachers—one from the junior high which will soon be called a middle school, one from an elementary school, and my colleague in the English department, Sara Madden. If you are interested, I may ask one or two other people. Anyone else in social studies that you would recommend?"

"Yah, there are," Megan said. "Are there any men in the group? I am assuming there are."

"No, there aren't."

"Why not?"

"Well, I didn't think about the fact that there are only women in the group," Cheryl admitted. "Men prefer their own book club. Also, as an English teacher, I have seen over the years that guys read different books than women. For example, my husband, Cliff, would never read what I read."

"Cheryl, the fact that Cliff reads different books than you do is the reason to integrate the book club," Megan explained. "Men reading different books than women do is precisely the point and the reason we should share literature with each other.

"Mary Wollstonecraft in her *A Vindication of the Rights of Woman* contended that men and women should share information and knowledge. She argued that the problem with the sexes is that men and women read different texts thus leading to greater separation between and among us. So, I wouldn't want to be a party to anything that further separates and segregates men and women or separates anyone else any further than we already are.

"A single-sex book club leads to more division which is precisely the problem as I see it. Having just women or just men in any club is splitting men and women from each other which I cannot abide. If the sexes would

197

just talk with—not to—but with each other, then we could understand each other better.

"It is like segregating the races or segregating by ages. How are we ever going to desegregate society if we don't talk with each other? And books are important to talk about communally.

"Just like some churches are segregated by race on Sundays, book groups separate the sexes on book club nights. I just can't participate in an event that segregates or even self-segregates any group of people. Sorry, Cheryl," Megan finished.

"I must admit that I have not thought about this, and maybe I ought to. Perhaps we should start an afterschool book club for our students. Would you be in favor of that?" Cheryl asked

"If we do that then I am for it as long as it is integrated."

"I get it, Megan. I get it."

In the teacher's lounge, I overheard Megan and Cheryl talking about the proposed book club and Megan's concern about including men. I asked them, "Megan and Cheryl, how about discussing the issue of most book clubs or other groups being segregated either by gender or race at our next Friday night potluck dinner?"

"Great idea, Mark. I am all in for the potluck with segregated book clubs as the issue," Cheryl said. "How about you, Megan?"

"I am in too," Megan agreed. "Let's discuss the issue over drinks and food. As you both know, I am against any kind of segregation—legal or just because it happens that way."

"What do you mean by 'just because?'" I asked.

"Well, Mark, it is the 'just so happens' excuse—'just because'—that these things 'just happen.' An example would be a group that has members from just one race,

religion, or sex only to run out of room for anyone else—
'SORRY!'

"The group's waiting list is also composed of the
'favored' group and then there is the 'no more room at
the inn' cliché. That is so phony—a group loads up with
just one kind of people then they say there is no room
BECAUSE—just because. Yah, sure, the explanation
goes 'Now there isn't any opening in our book club
because we have already stacked the group with people
we want in the group, which means not you.' What a
bunch of bull. There are so many ways to segregate like
this and I won't be a party to it," Megan stated.

I told Ana about the book club topic for a potluck
discussion. Ana said, "Let's do it, Mark. I would love
to hear what others think. Megan, as usual, has some
strong views. It should make for an interesting evening."

We scheduled a potluck dinner for March 22, 1996,
with John Browne, Megan Straffa, Zack Barber, Charles
Yates, Cheryl Wattsen, Lacey Walsh, April Danniels,
Jake Spanner, Claudia Pace, and Karla Betts.

I started the discussion, "Cheryl and Megan, you
have been talking about forming a book club. I think the
rest of our group would be interested in hearing about
your efforts. What kind of a book club do you want to
have and what kinds of books would you be reading?"

"What we would read is not as important to me as who
is in the book club," Megan explained. "As I told Cheryl,
for me to participate the group needs to be integrated
and be open to anyone from any background who wants
to read and discuss literature with a group."

"Hmmm, Megan, that is an interesting, and I must
say, a provocative position. In fact, after our earlier
discussion in the teacher's room I checked and found
that most book clubs are segregated—either by race or
gender. Cheryl, what is your view on that?" I asked.

"I am not sure anymore. The question that has been bothering me is: What do we do if our potential group members object to some other members?" Cheryl challenged. "More specifically, what if some of our potential members will not participate if there are men in the club? They might argue that men talk too much and dominate discussions. I have heard that argument from possible members of the group. So, like I said, I am not sure what to think. I understand what Megan is saying, but I am uncertain if integration will work."

"I think we need to make it work," Megan argued. "As I have indicated, I would like to have an integrated group of men and women—a racial mix, young and old, and rainbow. Together, we can learn to live with and love each other. I believe that being together and talking about books with each other results in the development of civil discourse. So, what are we afraid of?"

"Megan, you are using the words 'love' and 'civil'— it does not sound like you," Charles quipped. "What a surprise."

"Oh, Charles, you are so tiresome. You are trying to get on my nerves again, and this time I won't let it happen."

"Megan, what if I want to join the book group? You said you wanted men in the group."

"Actually, Charles, I would love to have you in a book group where you would read something other than the propaganda you generally consume."

"Yah, Megan, propaganda to you. Truth to me."

"But, Megan, what if men won't join?" Cheryl asked.

"They will, Cheryl," Megan insisted. "They will. But if they choose not to then that is up to them. I want them to have a choice if they want to join. We need to make it clear that we want them, and we have room for them."

"Even me, Megan?" Charles joked.

"Yes, Charles," Megan agreed, "even you."

"Well, I am ready and willing."

"I think we need to find readers who are different from us and invite them to join," Megan suggested. "In that way we can make it clear that they are welcome. A male friend of mine once tried to join a book club that had only women. The club organizer said there was a waiting list in front of him—all female. She told my friend that there wasn't a chance there would be an opening for him in the next couple of years, so he 'needn't bother getting on the list.' How is that for discouragement? In so many words, she said he was not welcome. Is blocking participation the way to help men and women understand each other?"

"I hear what you are saying, Megan," Cheryl said, "but it is not segregation if people choose to be with those they want to be with. We women don't want to be dominated by men. That isn't segregation—is it?"

"Oh, come on, Cheryl. We won't let anyone—men or anyone else—dominate our book club. I don't believe they will and if they try, we won't let them," Megan declared. "We will share time with them. No one will be allowed to direct the discussion; it will be free flowing. In addition, men might learn to appreciate our brains more than our bodies. That would be revolutionary. It's worth a try."

"Okay, Megan, I believe we should give it a try," John said. "I am ready to join with you and Cheryl and others. I would be a 'two-for'—I am black, and I am a male. What do you think?"

"Of course, John. I am all for it and glad you want to be in the club with us. You will add an important perspective. Let's give it a try. Hey, Cheryl, and everyone, men and women discussing books together is, as I said, REVOLUTIONARY! Bailey High's nickname is the 'Revs.' We could call the club, 'The Revs' Book Club.'"

"Megan, that is a bit corny, but I like it," Cheryl said. "Now, once the club gets going, we will have to confront the tough issues: Who chooses the books? From which genres? How many people should we have in our book club? How do we decide the number of participants? Where should we hold our meetings? How will we proceed when we meet? When do we decide on our process?" Cheryl asked.

"This is more difficult than I thought," John admitted.

"Yes, John," Cheryl agreed, "it is."

Chapter 22: "Money"

"Thank you all for coming," I said, beginning a professional development day session on media literacy for Gorham school district teachers. "I have talked with Lacey Walsh about today's session. Lacey and I agreed that telling personal stories will help us understand what goes on behind the scenes in the television industry. The details Lacey provides should help us in teaching media literacy to our students. So, Lacey, it is all yours."

"Hi everyone, as you have heard from Mark, my name is Lacey Walsh, I teach social studies and media literacy courses at Bailey High," Lacey said. "I would like this session to be interactive. So, please, when you have something to say, just jump in. Also, questions are welcome at any time.

"The basic concept about commercial television I need to start with is that it is about money, money, and more money. I realize that is a crass statement, but it helps us to understand why the medium does what it does.

"For example, when I worked in the television business, we splashed bright graphics on spinning screens to signal that we had 'Breaking News.' Of course, we did this to get the viewers' attention, and only secondarily to inform them. A commercial television network is a business enterprise. Its purpose is to keep viewers attentive long enough, so the commercials sell products. Our task as broadcasters was to entice, or to use the television producer's word, 'hook' the viewers into watching the commercials. The commercials prodded viewers into purchasing the advertised products.

"We 'teased' viewers at the beginning of a telecast by alerting them to 'Breaking News.' This technique kept viewers watching and waiting even when there was no news breaking.

"Breaking news follows the 'Soap Opera' formula of giving viewers a 'reward' every three to four minutes. It works. Television research indicates that viewers stay tuned even when there is no good reason to do so— except the knowledge that the reward is coming—after the commercial.

"When consumers purchase the advertised product, the objective is accomplished. Thus, we all make money—the television stations, the advertisers, and the retailers. Although high ratings and selling products in stores are usually correlated, we could have low ratings and stay employed if we were still selling products.

"Our final job on a newscast is to keep viewers 'tuned in' for the next show so they will consume more commercials urging—usually successfully—the consumption of more products.

"Megan Straffa, you have a question."

"Yes, I do," Megan said. "Are you saying, Lacey, you and your colleagues basically performed as conduits to sell 'goods?'"

"The short answer, Megan, is yes," Lacey admitted. "However, it is more complicated than that. I had some good colleagues—good reporters and such. Most of these professional men and women did not want to play the game. However, they realized that to get any news out at all they had to look good and attract attention through captivating visuals."

"Lacey, unfortunately, I think I get it. It isn't about informing the public as much as it is about selling products. That nauseates me," Megan said.

"Yah, television is a visual medium with sound used to enforce the picture," Lacey explained. "So, to get a story on the air you have to use visuals that attract attention. The alluring visuals often occlude the real story.

"A lot of important and complicated stories need words to be understood. The problem is that in television visuals invariably trump the words of a story. If visuals didn't dominate, then the visuals would be an unnecessary and an expensive addition to the program. Advertisers could save money by using less expensive radio commercials. However, they use the more expensive medium of television because the visuals are more effective than just sound.

"The important information—the material that matters in news reports that actually informs—is contained in the words. The visuals should complement a story, but on television pictures override the words. As a result, the substantive content gets lost.

"A more substantive way to obtain information is through reading because reading print is an active act; viewing television is passive. The book reader is in control; the viewer is not."

"Tell us more about the television business," I said.

"After spending time working in a television newsroom," Lacey went on, "I realized that I had to hype things and spike stories so viewers would keep watching through the intervening—but all important to the television station's economic well-being—

commercials. I also realized that my bosses wanted the viewers watching me AND the commercials.

"The experienced reporters just did it—sensationalized things. After a while, we didn't even have to think about it. We just did it. We were robotic and knew intuitively that above all else 'news' is a commercial enterprise and our job is to keep people watching. As I mentioned earlier, 'Breaking News' was not necessarily breaking. It was a gadget—a hook, if you will. It was our way of getting viewers to watch in preparation for the commercials."

"How could you and those good reporters you mentioned stand it?" Cheryl Wattsen asked.

"As I said before, if you were on the air and you attracted viewers, then the money you were paid was way more than anyone should be making for reading a script off a teleprompter.

"We received the amounts of money that bought us, as television personalities, nice cars to drive to our luxurious living accommodations. We had expense accounts with multiple credit cards and wore expensive clothes. In addition, there was some prestige in being a television star. The community fawned over me and other television personalities.

"If you were on television, your friends and family thought it was a big deal. Also, I received honoraria now and then for speeches, being a master of ceremonies, serving as a corporate board member, chairing this or that, and I was asked to write a book."

"I hope you write the book," Cheryl said.

"After I do some teaching, I think I will," Lacey said, "and, Cheryl, I assure you it will be my own book, not the one the managers would want me to write."

"You and April Danniels have a lot to communicate to us and the rest of the world."

"Please continue, Lacey," I said. "You are providing us with important behind-the-scenes information that we can communicate to our students."

"Sure. As a television personality, the benefits and the extras helped to pay for good wine along with Mediterranean and Caribbean cruises. At least, they did when I was able to take a vacation. Some of the bosses conflated taking vacations with not being committed enough to the mission."

"To clarify, the mission was to get viewers to the commercials which is the way television makes money. Is that right?" I asked.

"Yes, though, I need to say again that not everyone bought into the charade. I worked with some people who tried to deliver the news without sensationalizing stories on the way to the commercials."

"Didn't your conscience bother you?" Cheryl asked.

"Yes, it did occasionally when I was—shall we say— 'performing.' Now that I know what I was doing, my conscience really does bother me. When I write that book someday maybe you could read it before I send it to a potential publisher, Cheryl."

"You got it, Lacey. I would love to. I want to read yours and April's."

"Back to the benefits. You were talking about those," Megan said.

"Yes, Megan, there were some benefits. In fact, there were a lot of benefits, but they were mostly material— self-esteem was not one of the benefits.

"I received what was considered public esteem, but it did not leave me with personal esteem or self-respect."

"Lacey, I am still not getting it," I said. "Why would you give up the large amount of money you received, the exotic trips, the public recognition and so forth to become a teacher."

"Okay, Mark, I will explain why I wanted to become a teacher, but I must first be honest with you, Cheryl, and everyone at this workshop, as to why I left television.

"Even though it may sound trivial, my motivation for leaving the television industry is important to me. I left, in part, because I did not have a 'baby bump.'"

"What? I really don't get that explanation, Lacey. You are going to have to explain this one to me and, I believe, the rest of us," I said.

"Before I tell you about the baby bump quandary, I want to identify another thing about working at the station, which I think is relevant to my wanting to leave."

"We are listening," I said.

"Well, I got sick and tired of being hit on. As I told Mark and Cheryl in the interview meeting, there was some baggage that went with being considered 'hot,'" Lacey explained. "I was hit on all the time and sexist comments—veiled and not so veiled—were filtered even through some of the editorial discussions. The comments were considered smart, cute, humorous, and were deemed to be innocent. I didn't see them that way. If I found the comments out of bounds and said something, then the non-verbal response transmitted to me was, 'What's your problem lady?'

"The baby bump affront also got to me. A few of these guys—not many, but a few—had impregnated women. They married some of these women, and others they didn't. Then these predators would move on to the next woman—of course—sans baby bumps. I was one of those without a baby bump, so some of them moved on me. However, when I get married and have a baby, I will proudly show off my baby bump and those predators will stay away from me. Hooooray!"

"What did you do when you were hit on?" Megan

asked.

"Not as much as I should have. It was weird," Lacey admitted. "There were some men in higher management who were asexual. Even so, they had that look when they examined me. It gave me that uncomfortable feeling. They wouldn't necessarily do anything, but it was clear that they were visually undressing me. Also, they seemed to get their kicks out of saying stuff."

"Stuff—like what?" Megan inquired.

"I would overhear them when they would refer to me and other women as 'pieces of art.' We knew what they meant. They did not use the word ass, but they didn't have to. Even though they would not touch me intimately in public where there could be witnesses, I knew what they were thinking. This was all very uncomfortable.

"These managers were dirty old men, and some were dirty young men. They disgusted me. Men in the organization who wanted more than a furtive glance and a 'wet dream' bumped into me with their hands brushing my body.

"Some of these guys would put their arms around me as they whispered how much I would enjoy being with them. They not only wanted to be stroked verbally and told how wonderful they were, but some of them made it clear that they wanted to be caressed physically. The predators were more serious than the asexual ones. Both turned me off completely."

"Did you kick any of them in the balls?" Megan asked.

"No, I didn't, but I thought about it. I should have, but I didn't. So, to answer your earlier question, Megan, I didn't do much at all. I guess I was afraid of losing all the goodies I was receiving. The list of those I should have given a piece of my mind and a swift-kick continued growing.

"When I was deciding whether to leave my job, a guy confided in me, 'Well, Lacey, you know why you were hired, don't you?' I responded that I was not sure what he meant. My so-called friend and confidant then said, 'Lacey, it is because of what you look like. Like it or not, you are a dish.' He made it clear to me that it wasn't what I know that got me on the air in the first place or my knowledge that kept me there—it was what I looked like."

"Did you place him on your list after that comment?" Megan asked.

"Immediately."

"Lacey, now you are into teaching?"

"Yes, I am. I am proud of it."

"Are you ever going to tell your former boss and the rest of them how you felt being treated like an object?"

"Yes, Megan and everyone, once I get more settled into teaching, I am going to write Harold Marshlowe a note and ask him to spread the message."

"Who is that?" I asked.

"He was my boss. He was a suit—a colorless suit. He never wore anything else. There was nothing interesting about him. He did not vary in any way from one day to the next—black suits on Monday, Tuesday, Wednesday, Thursday, and Friday. When I saw him on weekends at business and social events, he was dressed even then in his customary funereal black."

"He sounds bland. When you confront him, what are you going to say?" Megan asked.

"Well, Marshlowe said he never read fiction, but his network delivered it every day through distorting events to attract viewers.

"So, if I see him, which I hope I never do, I will tell him that the network he directed sensationalized things drawing viewers to sell ads to make more and more dollars. He called it 'news,' but it was fluff. So, everyone, someday I will make the fiction and fluff comment to him. I will also tell him that I did not appreciate him ogling me all the time and telling me that I was a 'cutie.' That bastard."

"Lacey, I see you feel strongly about what happened to you in the television business," John Browne said.

"Yes, John. Yes, indeed. You have probably felt some of those same abuses. I can't imagine what it is like to be black in this society, and if you are black and a woman, it is double whammy—maybe even a triple whammy. Furthermore, in treating people of color, the network was a plantation.

"I realize saying the station was and still is a plantation is a strong statement, but that is what I was thinking while I was employed there and even more so since I left. Furthermore, there were not many African Americans at the network, Latinos, or other minority groups—certainly not in upper management where even when the MAN was a woman, the man ruled.

"Some minorities made it on-air when there was public pressure. When the pressure was off, the minorities were let go or reassigned to a lesser position. It was a white man's world with female accomplices who enabled their male benefactors.

"The male bosses realized they had to look like they were inclusive. They placed women in positions that looked like 'power,' but everyone knew who had the power."

"Lacey, would you teach our students about what you have recounted to us today?" I asked.

"Yes, Mark, I would," Lacey said. "With some judicious editing for age-appropriateness, I would teach what I have experienced and know to be the way it is in the 'real' world. I believe knowing what we talked about today will help students become media literate and more engaged citizens—that is why I want to teach."

Chapter 23: Alex

We had students like Alex Cooper in mind when we developed a media literacy curriculum for our students.

Alex binge-watched movies, one after another. He saw them mostly at home on the largest television screen his family could afford. He branded himself the "king of the marathon." Those who knew him agreed.

The nickname, King Marathon, wasn't always a compliment. The movies he delved into invariably involved the devil's combination of violence and sex.

Alex Cooper hunted for and then pursued violent movies in theatres. Walking to the theatre appeared to be his only exercise. Prior to choosing a seat, he purchased a giant sugared-drink, large popcorn with extra butter, and a candy bar or two.

As faculty, we had an obligation to help students like Alex think about what they were watching and what they were doing with their time.

I wrote to the faculty, "We ought to develop a way to deal with the students in our midst who, like Alex Cooper, spend inordinate amounts of time just viewing video after video. We must help these students study how the various media affect them. As educators, we should face the problem rather than ignore it. The various mass media are part of our students' lives. Therefore, we must confront the ubiquitous media and their residual effects. It is our responsibility to help our students become media literate."

Ms. L. designed a lesson plan to involve the students in media literacy studies. Doing so, she believed, "would help students become independent thinkers and active citizens with two 'thinking eyes.'" She went on to explain, "We should start by showing the students advertisements, and then ask, 'What are the advertisements selling?' This should be relevant for the students. They watch a lot of advertisements."

Lacey Walsh taught a sample class, recorded it, and showed it to interested faculty members. In teaching about ads, she asked students in the recorded class the following questions:

"To whom are they selling?"

A student responded, "They are selling to potential consumers, including us."

She asked, "How are they trying to sell the product?"

Another student commented, "They are selling to us through any avenue they can get away with. They get us to watch by using fast-moving, dramatic graphics. The visually compelling programming employs appealing subject matter to keep us tuned in—readying us for the ads."

"Are the ads effective?" Ms. L. asked.

A student volunteered, "Yes, the highly-produced, catchy advertisements are getting us to buy what they are selling. For sure it is working. We are suckers."

For an assignment in Lacey Walsh's class, Alex composed an instructional film on "media literacy" based on information he had learned in her class.

In part because a fellow student had created the video,

it nurtured and ripened student thinking. A movie by a student for students sparked student interest in the development of their critical scrutiny.

Motivated by success and peer appreciation, Alex then put together a series of ads illustrating how women are used in commercials to sell products. In studying a sample of beer ads, he determined that women participated primarily in three roles. He explained, "Women appear in beer ads as sex objects without speaking parts, as bartenders mixing the drinks primarily for men with roving eyes, or as waitresses waiting on men."

Alex added, "I have found that more recently in ads, women initiate activity more often, but for the most part my study illustrates that women still are all too frequently portrayed passively in television ads especially during sporting events which are mainly watched by men."

Learning from the activity, Alex did not want to see women objectified. In his presentations, he cautioned fellow students and faculty observers, "My mother and sister are not objects and should not be portrayed that way."

Lacey Walsh communicated to her students, "Producing media presentations is one of the best ways to learn about media literacy because you are involved in production and learn about angles, close ups, cuts, and a whole host of media manipulations."

In a meeting with faculty, Lacey said, "After learning how to produce presentations, learners will be able to discern what the producer is doing. As a result, students can protect themselves against being manipulated. In addition, students will be able to better enjoy a presentation because they know how it is put together."

Lacey Walsh helped the faculty see the importance of a student like Alex learning that "mixing beer advertisements with cars and trucks is a dangerous business, because mixing alcohol and driving is a bad idea. Alex had shown the class advertisements that made it look glamorous to drink beer juxtaposed with ads for automobiles."

Ms. L. continued, "Our students need to recognize what the commercials are selling and how they are making it seductive. We need to help our students be aware of the enticements. A fellow student, Alex, assisted his classmates in understanding what they see, hear and experience. If students are not thinking when watching television or movies, they could conflate the glamour of driving and owning expensive cars with the consumption of beer. Students who are not thinking for themselves unwittingly become mindless consumers.

"Alex Cooper illustrated the dangerous mix of drinking and driving. When Alex communicated with other students, he reinforced some of the points I have been making with the students, but in language that his fellow students understand."

After the earlier discussions Ms. L and Alex led on how the media creates news and advertisements to sell products, Lacey reported to the faculty, "The students began to recognize the ways in which television sells products, as well as politicians, to consumers and citizens—often using the same methods. Adlai Stevenson, the Democratic candidate for president in 1952, bemoaned television's ability to sell candidates like soap. Television sold politicians in the 1950s. The medium is still selling politicians and products."

Lacey added, "Television, and now the Internet, are selling young people's future purchasing power to advertisers. The technologies available to television producers are effective selling machines.

"As of the 1920s, radio provided advertisers a direct

wire into the homes of consumers. Prior to radio broadcasting, humans sold to consumers—sometimes house to house. Since the 1920s, a machine has done the selling job and still does. Television followed, and now the Internet. Educators need to work with students to help them control the technologies rather than the technologies controlling the students."

After a brief break, Lacey continued, "The National Football League's Super Bowl goes all day. This is after weeks-long hyperbole. Television provides a giant flea market for its advertisers. Ersatz controversy feeds viewers with concocted excitement because they are really not watching a football game. For example, and to bolster the point I am making, in a sixty-minute game the ball is only in motion for about twelve minutes. The clock keeps running during the game unless there are timeouts. In fact, the day long, indeed, week-long super bowl commercials basically sell products in an event disguised as a football game."

Ms. L. proceeded to report that her student, Vinnie, after doing some research, reported to his class, "By the time students reach their eighteenth birthday, the students will have seen one million ads just on television. One hundred thousand of those will be for beer. Watching game after game assures that the message gets to its targeted audience."

Lacey then told us, "I assigned students to analyze some television advertising during programs aimed at their age group and asked them: 'What are the commercials selling? To whom are they selling? Are the ads effective?'

"A student in my class responded, 'I would say they are effective. Also, Ms. L., they are selling a lifestyle, which most of us have bought into. As for aiming at potential beer drinkers, the ads are working on me, my friends, and almost everyone else.'

"Of course, I had to respond to that, I said, 'If you are watching those advertisements, I hope you don't drive and drink and if you are under-age you shouldn't drink at all.'"

Another student added, "Yes, Ms. L., they are getting us to buy what they are selling. For sure it is working. We fall for it. The marketing departments study who we are, what we want, and the cleverest methods to sell to us. They realize that we are so attentive to the pictures on the screen that we have stopped thinking for ourselves. We just soak it all in. The result—we buy what is advertised."

Lacey challenged our professional workshop group, "With our previous discussions on how the media creates news, and how they use advertisements to sell products, the students are beginning to see connections and making them. The question we need to ask ourselves is this: What effect does all of this advertising have on young people who do not have media literacy concepts and skills?"

Chapter 24: "PC"

Megan Straffa, Lacey Walsh, Charles Yates, April Danniels, Zack Barber, Claudia Pace, Jake Spanner, John Browne, Karla Betts, and Cheryl Wattsen attended a potluck dinner on Friday, September 26, 1997. Ana and I continued to host at our home.

I initiated our discussion, "Is political correctness becoming shorthand for restricting freedom of speech? What do you think?"

"First, Mark, I have a question: What is political correctness?" Jake inquired. "I want to make sure I have a definition before I respond. I have some other questions that I would like to ask, but first I need a definition that makes sense to me."

"Charles, you look like you want to respond," I said. "Do you have a definition?"

"Yes, Mark. Here is my definition: I define political correctness as avoiding saying something that you believe to be true because the statement might offend a person or a group of people," Charles explained.

"What are some examples of political correctness?" I asked.

"I believe saying something that could be perceived as racist or sexist."

"Why then, Charles, would political correctness be a problem if it is a matter of perception?"

"It is a problem, Mark, because people won't say things that they want to say or even that they should say because the statements might hurt someone's feelings," Charles argued. "Therefore, there is not a full discussion of important concerns. We don't get all points of view—just those considered politically correct."

"Charles, if I get what you are saying, people watch what they say. As a result, your point is that debate is shut down. You are arguing that those protesting PC have a point. Is that what you are contending?" I asked.

"Yes. I believe those protesting against politically correct speech have a point. We can't use the racial epithets about people or other words that are construed, but are not in fact, racist. We can't refer to a place as a 'ghetto' without defining in highly restrictive terms what is meant, or we need to exclude words that are perceived as synonyms for hateful terminology and deemed hurtful. If that is the case, then after a while we won't be saying anything to anyone."

"Do some of the 'language police' go too far?" Zack asked.

"Yes, Zack, unfortunately they do—way too far," Charles said.

"I would also like to answer that. As Charles and Zack have indicated, the language police do go too far," Claudia said. "If you have to worry about everything you say because you might offend someone about something, then there is little left to talk about."

"And then there are 'triggers' and 'trigger warnings,'" Charles exlplained. "I define triggers as using certain words that upset someone. Pretty soon we won't be saying anything to anyone about any subject. I have trouble calling that a free society."

"I am with Charles on this one. Let people talk. We are way too sensitive to perceived insults," Zack agreed.

"As a liberal, I agree with my Libertarian friend, Zack. The 'First Amendment' to the Constitution of the United States provides people with the right to be wrong. So, we need to fight bad speech with more speech. In general, the more speech the better. I realize the First Amendment does not give you license to pronounce libelous accusations. However, we should not shut people up just because they are wrong about something. If that were the case, then we would be silencing a lot of people. Instead, we need to open everyone's public comments to the light of day, so they can be scrutinized, and if need be—rebutted."

"I agree with what you just said, Jake. However, what can we say in class without getting into trouble?" Megan asked.

"Megan, Zack, Jake, and everyone else, we shouldn't worry about offending people," Claudia said. "We must teach and discuss what we believe to be true without fear.

"A robust teacher's union can help keep us out of trouble. Therefore, we need a strong union to defend us when we are attacked for doing our jobs. We need academic freedom in the classroom. A union will defend our freedom to teach. There is power in organizing, and especially if we have lots of members."

"Claudia, I agree. We need to take risks to help students learn, and I would like union protection," John said.

"In our classes, we must jolt our students out of their comfort zones. Indeed, we need to create cognitive dissonance in the classroom to spur our students into thinking.

"Some powerful individuals don't want us to challenge

221

students' prejudices. Those students who believe and spout propaganda OUGHT to get upset. However, there are some things students might say that should not be permissible."

"Like what, Megan, like what? You are contradicting yourself. It sounds like you are for censorship? Are you?" Charles asked.

"Well, I will tell you, Charles, there are some words students better not say in my presence."

"For example?"

"Do I really need to tell you, CHARLES?"

"Yes, please do."

"Okay, I will. Racist comments, derogatory statements about women, belittling people who have a different sexual orientation, and so forth. And, they better not call me 'honey,' or else."

"Hey, Megan, if I call you honey, what will the or else be?"

"Try it, Charles. Then I will ask the group to avert their eyes, and I will show you. You won't like it."

"Alright, Megan and Charles. Let's get back to the issue at hand," I said.

"When I am teaching, am I free to speak conservative thoughts in my classroom?" Charles asked. "I don't think soooo! You so-called progressives would go apoplectic if I did speak truth to liberal power."

"I do not think that is what happens, at least not in my classroom. In my classroom, all points of view are welcome," Claudia said. "I am not for censoring speech—just excluding insulting and harmful words from the classroom and purging them from written communication.

"You can't be against that, Charles. Are you? I believe you and others can say what you want to say, except when you say something that harms someone."

"Hurtful and harmful words to whom? What hurts one person may not hurt someone else. And, besides, who decides what is hurtful and what isn't?" Charles asked.

"I agree with Charles on this. I believe the less censorship the better. What he says makes sense. If we start eradicating words we don't like from spoken and written communication, then there won't be much left," Zack responded.

"Of course. you cannot say just anything you want to—especially, in the classroom. However, every little thing should not be a reason to stifle a teacher trying to teach," John said.

"How can we get students to think if we cannot use cognitive dissonance, and periodically say things that some would see as offensive?" Jake asked. "I believe we won't be able get students to think critically if we don't shake their preconceptions. We need to shake their intellectual trees to get them to see the other side. If we can't see the other side, then we are locked into the only argument we know. Indeed, there may be more than two sides in any debate of issues."

"On the question of language, students have asked me, 'Mr. M., is it okay to say black or should I say African American, or should I say something else? I don't want to offend anyone.' Students ask me that and similar questions frequently. I agree we have to create controversy in the classroom to get students thinking, but we shouldn't go too far and offend people," I said.

"Mark, how can we determine what will offend a student, a citizen in Gorham, or in any other place for that matter? What do we do if a student verbally abuses another? And, what if something a student says is offensive to us as teachers? What do we do then?" Jake asked. "When is political correctness a barrier to

223

considering ideas that are uncomfortable, but necessary to think about?"

Chapter 25: Paul

We needed a teacher to replace Vivian Todd. Vivian left Bailey High for another position in a community closer to her family. She taught courses in the social studies and history department. Vivian also had directed our new media center which incorporated the library.

The vacancy gave us a chance to hire a new teacher. I explained to our principal, Rose Drouin, "We aren't necessarily looking for someone who has been in the media. However, with the growth of cable television and additional news outlets, we could use additional help in developing our students' media literacy concepts and skills."

Principal Drouin recommended and approved the search for a teacher who understood the new media, and how innovative technologies were affecting our students.

Because cultural and social media were expanding, Lacey Walsh had developed media literacy units to discuss its impact. A new teacher could bridge teaching courses in social studies, media, and English.

We interviewed Paul O'Bien who possessed the knowledge and skills we were looking for. He had been involved in the media and had political experience as well. If we hired Paul, his background would augment Lacey Walsh's experience in television, and Angela Tremonte's background in politics.

After interviewing Paul O'Bien, we proposed to the Gorham district office that he be hired. The district offered him the job. Paul accepted and became Mr. P.

Paul had studied candidates campaigning for the presidency. He and his co-author wrote about the candidates' preparation and performance in televised debates. His work helped those seeking election appear proficient and competent on television, which was the primary medium voters used to gather information about presidential candidates.

Bailey High's social studies and history faculty expected that as a member of our faculty, Paul would use his experiences to assist other faculty by conveying what he knew to our students.

As with Lacey Walsh, Paul had decided to change professions. He had a variety of reasons for doing so.

Paul's parents had lived in Nebraska since birth. They were rabid University of Nebraska Cornhusker fans. In the fall, they scheduled their weeks around Saturday's games. The family attended home games, and assembled around the television set for away games. When the university played in bowl games, family tradition held that at least two members of the O'Bien clan attend.

Paul's family worked the ancestral farm. The three oldest children entered and graduated from state colleges. Paul was big enough at six feet and two hundred pounds to play high school football, but not big or fast enough to play in college, especially at a division one school like Nebraska.

The fourth child in the family, and like his two

brothers and sister, Paul always planned to go to college. Unlike his siblings, he chose to study in the northeast. Paul earned grades and test scores high enough to earn an academic scholarship. In college, he double-majored in political science and history, minored in radio and television, and took supporting courses in English.

While in college in Connecticut, Paul O'Bien met Darlene Price, a native of New Hampshire. Paul and Darlene dated in college. Both were interested in politics and took several of the same courses together. In the fall semester of 1991, Darlene and Paul took time off from school to conduct research on the New Hampshire presidential preference primary. Specifically, they studied how candidates exhibited themselves on television. In the process, they learned enough to joint-author a paper for a college class. Their professor found the paper perceptive, and asked if he could circulate it to others. Paul and Darlene agreed.

Staff for some of the candidates for president in the 1992 presidential elections used Darlene and Paul's paper to groom candidates for television appearances. The term paper advised staff of presidential candidates how to coach their respective candidates to look good on television. The paper also informed the candidates themselves on how to prepare for and present themselves during presidential debates.

Paul and Darlene resolved they would forego participating in political campaigns directly; rather, they circulated what they had learned to all candidates, and to the public, so readers could ascertain how television affects presidential debates.

In developing the paper, Darlene and Paul studied the extant video from all the previous televised presidential debates. The researchers began with the 1960 contest between John F. Kennedy, the Democratic nominee, and Richard M. Nixon, the Republican nominee. When viewing the videos, it was clear to Darlene and Paul that Kennedy understood television and its impact on viewers much better than Nixon did.

Kennedy later said it was television that helped him become the president of the United States. The authors indicated, "Kennedy's eyes penetrated the camera directly into the nation's living rooms. Nixon's eye movements circled the screen generating a candidate who looked shifty and untrustworthy—not something any candidate for the presidency intends."

Darlene and Paul asserted, "It is more what you look like on television than what you say or what anyone says about you that makes the difference in who is elected. What the candidate says matters, but it is of secondary importance. The visuals convey the messages that get through to the viewers

"If, therefore, it is what you look like that gets you elected, then this has profound implications for a country that calls itself a democracy. In a democracy, voters claim they elect candidates based on what they stand for rather than visual peripherals. The 1960 presidential election belies the claim. Indeed, in 1960, Kennedy looked stately and poised on television. His tanned face, dark suit, and vertical features fit handsomely inside a television screen.

"Prior to the first debate, Kennedy trailed Nixon in the opinion polls. After his performance in the first presidential debate on September 26, 1960, Kennedy inched ahead and stayed in front to become the president of the United States in a close election. Kennedy may have been the best candidate to become president, but being the best looking on television ought not be the main criterion."

Paul and Darlene wrote, "There were no presidential

debates in 1964, 1968, and in 1972. In 1964, the incumbent president, Lyndon B. Johnson, did not want to give the Republican nominee, Senator Barry Goldwater from Arizona, the same chance Richard Nixon had given John F. Kennedy in 1960. Johnson won in an electoral college landslide in 1964 vindicating his politically strategic decision not to debate.

"In 1968, Nixon demonstrated he had learned from having provided Kennedy an opportunity to defeat him. Consequently, Nixon did not give the Democratic nominee in 1968, Hubert H. Humphrey, the chance Nixon had given Kennedy in 1960. Nixon won in 1968.

"Four years later, Nixon again declined to debate his opponent, George McGovern, the Democratic nominee. The incumbent president won in a landslide."

Paul and Darlene renewed their analysis of the presidential debates when televised debates resumed in 1976. "On October 6, 1976, President Gerald Ford, the unelected incumbent, debated Democrat Jimmy Carter. In their consequential second of three presidential debates, sixty-four million people watched the encounter as President Gerald Ford made a comment about Eastern Europe that was difficult to understand. Because of Ford's perplexing response to a question, some members of the media characterized President Ford's response as a mistake. The election in the Electoral College was close, 297 electoral votes for Carter to 240 for Ford. Consequently, Jimmy Carter became president of the United States. The characterization of the debate by some in the media may have been decisive in the 1976 election."

About the still-discussed 1980 debates, Darlene and Paul wrote, "In 1980, Ronald Reagan, the Republican nominee for president, debated the incumbent, President Carter. Reagan had experience in using the media and it showed during his October 28, 1980, debate with Jimmy Carter. Reagan maintained direct eye contact with the camera. His 'There you go again' one-liner elicited laughter from the crowd. Reagan's media skills did Carter in. On national television, where visuals are all important, Reagan 'looked' in control—Carter did not. Reagan won in the electoral college, 489 to 49. Reagan gained almost 10 percent more popular votes than did Carter which resulted in Republicans gaining control of the United States Senate and adding members in the House of Representatives."

In President Ronald Reagan's bid for re-election, Darlene and Paul explained, "In 1984, Democrat Walter Mondale challenged President Reagan. In the first debate, Reagan was ineffective. However, in the second debate on October 21, 1984, Reagan delivered another classic one-liner." Darlene and Paul wrote, "After the first debate, many commentators in the various media cited Reagan's age as a potential problem. In the second debate, Reagan turned the age-table on Mondale by saying, 'I am not going to exploit, for political purposes, my opponent's youth and inexperience.' The sound bite played over and over in subsequent days on various television networks' news reports. Reagan won decisively."

In the 1988 presidential debate, Paul and Darlene illustrated, "Once again the well-coached Republican candidate, this time George H. W. Bush, out-performed a Democratic candidate, Michael Dukakis."

By the early 1990s, Darlene Price and Paul O'Bien were ready and willing to communicate to anyone who would listen what they had learned studying presidential debates.

The Democratic candidate for president in 1992, William J. Clinton, did not need to be told where the cameras were—he knew. Growing in the television era, Clinton understood how to make eye contact directly through the camera to voters sitting watching television in their living rooms. Clinton skillfully delivered one-liners. President George W. Bush, the incumbent, appeared to have forgotten what he had learned in 1988. Bush's media advisers in 1988 were no longer coaching him. He was on his own and a reaction shot of him checking his watch as if he were in a hurry to go somewhere proved his undoing.

Clinton recognized televised debates were performances. He realized capturing and dominating the stage gave the candidate a televisual-political advantage. Consequently, viewers observed Clinton roaming the dais—moving toward the audience. Television viewers watched Clinton rather than his opponent—visuals dominated. Clinton looked better on television and won twice.

Because of his televised dominance, Clinton ascended to the presidency in 1992. He won re-election in 1996 using the same television principles he had used in 1992.

Students at Bailey High read and discussed in their social studies and English classes the dystopian novels, George Orwell's *1984* and Aldous Huxley's *Brave New World*. The books foretold a dominion replete with "tele-screens" and "feelies." As the twentieth century dawned, I asked the Bailey High faculty, "Are our students ready as political television in the United States propels toward Orwell's and Huxley's forecasts?"

Chapter 26: Panther

"Mark, who is the 'panther?'" Ana asked me one day.

"Huh?"

"The student they call the 'Black Panther,'" she repeated. "Who is it?"

Few African American families and students lived in Gorham, Massachusetts. Traditionally, and like some other New England communities, people segregated based on who they wanted their neighbors to be. This usually meant the desire to live near those like themselves. Adding to the ethnic separation, intentional or not, the historic patterns of segregation also divided people based on their income.

The families with fewer resources resided in Gorham, but they populated the sump-pumped lowland area on the other side of the river. If a family did not have a car, the family's children walked to school. When the bridges flooded and washed out the pathways, the students found their ways to school any way they could.

Without personal transportation, the adults searched for ways to work. Public transportation in Gorham was unreliable; the buses showed up when they showed up.

Ana's mixed parentage had been accepted in Gorham

as long as we did not move too close to the wealthier parts of town. We lived "down-wind" where real estate prices were cheaper and pollution greater. The higher-priced properties were in the northwest part of town; the prevailing winds blew polluted particles elsewhere.

The prejudice against minorities moving into the wealthier neighborhoods was cloaked in a protecting "property values" rationale: "We aren't against 'those' people moving into our part of town as long as they will keep up their property which will maintain the value of our property." This was generally followed by, "But they don't keep up their property—therefore, just keep 'them' where they are among their own people and we will all be happy. They can come into our part of town after we sell our houses for good prices, retire, and move to Florida, Texas, or Arizona."

In addition to the river separating us, Gorham's white supremacists intended to keep things the way they had been historically. The town's racism manifested itself covertly, periodically bubbling to the surface.

The fact that Ana taught in town and was married to a white man made some in Gorham uncomfortable. For those residents, it was okay for us to be married provided we did not get too close to their section of town.

Ana and I did not have the resources to live in the wealthier part of town, and even if we did have the money, we preferred living where we had originally chosen. In our community, we lived with folks like us—diverse and accepting regardless the background. We accepted each other for who were rather than for what we owned. The entrenched powers had little to worry about because we, and other minority families, seldom thought about moving into the northwest part of town where housing was expensive, the residents homogeneous, and "the other" unwelcome.

Gorham's citizens expected the schools to reinforce its social mores and political ideology. There could be a difference of opinion, but not much.

In one of Jake Spanner's history classes, Mr. J. had Michael Jonnes as a student. Like Ana, Michael was of mixed heritage.

Michael immersed himself in United States history. He learned the traditional history—celebratory and white-male. However, Michael also learned about the history of African Americans and other minority groups. As a result, he wanted others to know about all facets of the history of the United States including the history of those who had been disenfranchised.

Although he lifted weights and had built himself up, Michael never used his strength and size to get his way. Nicknamed GG, the gentle giant, he used the power of evidence-anchored arguments to persuade.

In Jake's class, Michael wrote a term paper about the "Black Panthers." He contended, "Black Panthers actively tried to bring about change in the United States from the middle 1960s to the early 1980s. The Black Panthers generated controversy wherever they went."

According to Michael, "The Panthers monitored the police in an attempt to make sure the police did not abuse residents in black communities." He wrote further, "The Panthers created community programs intended to feed, clothe, educate, and organize residents." He posited, "The last thing the white hierarchy wanted was for blacks to become powerful politically and self-sufficient economically. Black economic independence would remove an exploited source of cheap labor. Black political power could challenge the white elite's dominance—a frightening prospect to the power structure."

Michael noted further, "Some government officials

believe the Black Panthers was a radical group. Because of this belief, the police spied on the Black Panthers. Even though the group knew this, undercover police were able to infiltrate and destabilize Black Panther organizations."

In his essay, Michael maintained, "The Black Panthers helped their respective communities. Therefore, law enforcement targeted this group because they attempted to help black citizens." He concluded his paper: "The evidence supports my conclusion that the Black Panthers as an organization tried to help black communities and black people. Law enforcement officers targeted the Panthers because it was perceived that they were a radical group." Then Michael's last sentence summarized his thesis, "The Panthers were not a radical group unless you believe trying to help black people is a radical act."

Michael submitted his paper to his United States history teacher, Jake Spanner. Michael also shared his text with other students.

Gorham's lone underground newspaper, "Gorham Exposed," acquired a copy of Michael's paper and published it in its entirety. Because of the publication of his work, Michael's overall thesis that the Black Panthers influence on black communities was intended to be positive gained the attention of Gorham's more conservative citizens. That is when, as Megan Straffa said, "All hell broke loose. Gorham's reactionary citizenry unhinged, and the town's cloaked racism unmasked."

Some adults in the community hurled racial epithets in Michael's direction after the publication of his writing. Upon reading the article, Blake Desmond, a school board member, telephoned Bailey High demanding that Michael apologize and, "the article be withdrawn, and the teacher disciplined who had, shall I say charitably, that youth in class. If the teacher helped the student write the paper in any way, the teacher should be fired or, at the very least, suspended and his pay docked until the teacher recognizes what he did was wrong and promises to never assign and accept such trash again. He should then apologize to Bailey High School, the Gorham community and the school board. And, only then—after an apology—should he be able to enter Bailey T. S. Memorial High School again."

Mr. Desmond further claimed that "the paper should never have been written, and that teacher Jake Spanner should not have let the paper see the light of day or encouraged the student to write it."

Inflaming the critics even more was Jake's award of an A for the paper, and Mr. J's comment on the paper that Michael's "brilliant analysis and solidly researched conclusion merits wide-distribution."

Gorham's reactionary citizenry wanted vengeance. Ana and I announced an impromptu potluck for Friday, February 27, 1998. We planned to discuss the issue of Michael Jonnes' paper and a school board member's demand that Jake Spanner be disciplined.

After we assembled with food and drink, I asked, "What should we do about Michael's paper and school board member Blake Desmond's call for its withdrawal. In addition, Mr. Desmond has demanded a reprimand for both Michael Jonnes and Jake Spanner. Jake is with us tonight. What do you all think?"

"Screw Desmond," Megan said.

"Oh, come on Megan. What is your point?" Charles asked.

"Well, Charles, I will make it."

"Okay, go ahead and make it."

"Listen up then, Charles," Megan went on. "This is an

issue of academic freedom. As Jake said in his comment to Michael Jonnes, it is a well-researched paper. Michael drew warranted conclusions from the research. Are we supposed to withdraw papers that are carefully crafted because some powerful person in the community does not like the conclusion a student arrives at?

"If so, our school is a propaganda mill where our students can only arrive at the conclusions that conform to and are acceptable to the politically powerful in Gorham. If that is the case, and Gorham is a model for the other schools in our state and country, then you cannot call the United States of America a free country because only certain beliefs are accepted. That is tyranny, and the call for the paper's withdrawal is fascistic," Megan exclaimed.

"Megan, you are again calling something fascism, which is a habit of yours. Doing so is a little strong or a lot strong don't you think?" Charles said smirking.

"Once again, Charles, you are belittling what I am saying. You, as a teacher, should be on my side on this one," Megan argued. "Fascism occurs when there is corporate control. The controllers use police and the military to enforce corporate policies, and as a result we have an autocratic government. Sounds like Gorham to me."

"Megan, I need more details. I am with Charles on this one that what you are saying is too extreme," I said.

"Fair enough, Mark. Although the school board is not a corporation, it tries to control what we do and what the students think. Our country is moving in the direction of fascism. We must remain vigilant. The difference between an autocracy and democracy is thread-thin. Powerful groups can cut the thread."

"Megan, once again you are exaggerating, and you are way over the top. Your analysis is a bizarre analysis by an extremist—YOU, Megan, YOU! You are the extremist bordering on radicalism. In fact, you may have already crossed-over.

"I hope no one else hears what you are saying here tonight. Your comments are way out of bounds, as they often are, and, I must say, un-American. Using the term fascism is the socialist's way of condemning our system. I have heard socialist talk from this group in the past, and now I am hearing this fascism crap. Don't you think, Megan, that once again you are going way too far in your condemnation of what we do here in Gorham and in this country?" Charles pleaded.

"Damn it, Charles," Megan said. "When a student can't write a paper and arrive at the conclusions that the student's research warrants, then what would you call that society? I would call it fascistic. And it is the fascistic society that you are defending that is un-American. The First Amendment has to matter more to us than what Blake Desmond wants done."

"But in this country, you can vote people out of office if you don't like their decisions."

"Oh, Charles, you have to know better than that. You know that the people who control this society have the money to elect people who do their bidding. The controllers in the United States have gerrymandered congressional districts for the powerful to win. In addition, the undemocratic Electoral College elects the president. The president is supposed to represent all of the people in this country but doesn't when elected by the Electoral College rather than the popular vote.

"The people in control have disenfranchised a host of different minority groups. Michael Jonnes pointed out inequities, which is why his paper and papers like it are so troublesome to the elite.

"Michael has revealed the truth. Maybe he did not

reach the whole truth or the part of the truth you would like, but anything that questions the present power structure rattles those in power and upsets you, Charles.

"Racism permeates our community. This is the land of the free—as long as you are white and male," Megan declared.

"Oh, Megan, come on."

"You can go out and change things if you don't like what is happening," Charles offered.

"Well, Charles," Megan said, "I might. I just might."

Chapter 27: "Choice"

"Hey Mark, how about we go teach in a charter school?" Zack offered. "Or, better still, create our own charter school.

"Since 1992, charter schools have been increasing in states where they are permitted. Charter schools could allow us to teach the way we want. We might be able to avoid the kinds of problems Jake Spanner ran into with Michael Jonnes and the 'Black Panther' paper."

"Zack, I have heard about charter schools, but I don't know that much about them," I admitted.

"Well, as a Libertarian, they make sense to me. Besides, you get to use public money to run a school. In addition, you have the freedom to teach your way."

"Ahh. Sounds good, maybe too good to be true. I am not sure what they are all about. I do realize charters are just beginning to become popular. So, Zack, how do they work?" I asked.

"I have been looking into charter schools because they fit with my libertarian philosophy," Zack explained. "In different states, there are various ways of creating charter schools and administering them.

"Basically, what you do is apply for a charter to a county or a state in states that permit charter schools.

In your application, you identify what you are trying to do. If the governing agency agrees that what you are trying to do fits into the requirements to start a charter school in a state, then you are provided with a charter and a certain amount of public money to run your school. What do you say, Mark? Sounds good doesn't it? Should we apply for a charter?"

"Zack, not so fast," I said. "Are you serious?"

"Actually I am. Why not start a charter school with public money? It is a great idea. How about it, Mark?"

"I would have to know a whole lot more about it. And, Zack, what is the difference between charter schools and vouchers? I have heard about both concepts, but the terminologies are new to me. How are they the same, and how are they different?"

"Mark, they are actually quite different," Zack explained. "In some states, vouchers can be used for private school tuition. The voucher acts like a check, but it comes from public funds and can be used for private school tuition in states where it is permitted. In a few of those states, vouchers can be used to pay tuition even if the schools are religious."

"You said vouchers can be used in parochial schools. Aren't there some First Amendment—church and state—issues when public money is used for religious education?" I asked. "And what happens to the public schools if parents and their students have a choice to go wherever they want to? Enrollments could drop so there would be less money for regular public schools."

"The theory is that the regular public schools will have to get better to compete with the choices parents and their children make," Zack said. "In a competitive system, regular public schools would have to improve to attract students. Sounds good doesn't it?

"Choice will provide for more winners. The public

schools will get better to compete."

"Not everyone will win, though. Will they?"

"No. Not everyone, of course, will win through choice. The good schools win, and the bad schools lose. In a free society, that is the way it should be. Isn't it?"

"But, Zack, what will happen to traditional public schools if people start using public money for these other options? It is common sense that there is only so much money to go around."

"The regular public schools either do an effective and efficient job at competently educating kids or they cease to exist," Zack said.

"Is that what we want in our society?" I inquired.

"Yes, some real competition. It is survival of the fittest. You either do the job or you don't. If you don't... well, GOODBYE!"

"Zack, how about if our next potluck dinner discusses this issue?"

"Cool. Let's do it."

At our Friday night potluck dinner on October 22, 1999, I opened our dinner discussion, "I have been learning about the concept of choice. Zack got me going on this. After studying the issue, I have found that various terms are used in the 'choice' lexicon—opportunity scholarships, vouchers, charter schools—but a lot of assumptions about education are inserted into the terminology. What do you all think?"

"The terminology 'choice' historically has been a synonym for segregation and still is in my judgment. That is what I think about this business of school choice. It is a Trojan horse. Buy into it, and then watch out—pretty soon everything in education is privatized for profit," Jake stated.

"Jake, you used the word business in describing choice, and I believe that is exactly what it is. It is one more way for business interests to take over our schools, and, as you said, it is a case of corporations using public money to make more money for private interests," Megan agreed.

She continued, "In addition to businesses gaining more control over our students' minds, parents using vouchers can basically take their kids out of integrated schools and place them in segregated, private, for-profit schools. After the 1954 Brown decision to integrate overrode the 1896 Plessy 'equal but separate' decision, I thought we were through with this stuff—guess not."

"I agree with Megan. We are finding ingenious ways to re-segregate schools. And this so called 'choice' movement is either consciously trying to segregate or they are blithely unaware of the unintended result. I am not for it. We already have enough ways in which we divide people," John Browne said.

"Oh, come on, John, what is wrong with giving parents and kids a choice? What, in hell, are we afraid of?" Zack asked.

"Zack, what I am afraid of is re-segregating schools and using public money to do so. The re-segregation will once again make the rich richer and the poor poorer. That is the last thing we need."

"Well, so be it. With what we are doing now, the poor kids are getting screwed anyway. How much worse can it get?"

"What you are saying, Zack, is that the screwed are always getting screwed. Why not try something new and screw them some more? The circular logic is ridiculous," Cheryl said.

"Sure, Zack and Cheryl, the folks with limited incomes are always getting screwed. So, what is new?" Megan asserted. "Fuck the system."

"I get the facetiousness of your comment, Megan. So,

what should we do now, Mark?" John said.

"I don't know, everyone. What is the answer?"

"Mark. We just need more choice. It is as simple as that," Zack argued.

"Zack, it is not that simple," Megan said. "Instead we should do the hard work of creating better public schools."

"It will never happen, Megan," John said. "Those who control things don't want it to happen."

"I hope you are wrong about that, John," I said.

Chapter 28: Suzie

"Mark, Suzie is so concerned about her weight. She is short like me. She looks fine to me, but she is concerned about what others think of her. She believes some kids at school are making fun of her when she walks by," Ana said.

"Ouch, as a father, if that is true, it really bothers me. Ana, maybe she is imagining things. At least, I hope she is."

"No, Mark, I don't believe she is. In fact, I am sure she isn't."

"If that is the case, that she is being bullied because of what she looks like, then that is awful," I said. "It hurts me to even think about what Suzie must be going through. Ana, it is a slap in the face, and it doesn't feel good—not good at all."

"It hurts me too, Mark," Ana agreed. "Thinking about what she must be experiencing cuts to my core. Ever since we got married and I gained some weight, I have worried now and then about my weight, but you have helped me through it by telling me how much you love me and that I look good to you."

"Not only do you look good to me. You are the most beautiful person in the world to me."

"I love you so much, Mark. I appreciate what you have said to me. But how can we help Suzie accept herself like we accept each other?"

"The fact that my daughter is going through something like this upsets me," I said, my voice breaking. "My confidence as a parent dissolves when I think Suzie is hurting. I hope we can help her deal with it."

"And, Mark, Suzie told me," Ana stopped mid-sentence, quivering before continuing, "'Mommie, when I walk down the halls, some kids say *Hi* to me.'"

"Honey, what is wrong with that? I don't get it. Why would that affect Suzie?"

"Well, Mark, Suzie cried when she said, 'They follow it with a B-R-I-D, because I am mixed race,'" Ana sobbed through her words.

"Ana. I don't get that either—B-R-I-D. I am not sure I understand—mixed race. What in hell is that all about?" I asked.

"Combined with 'hi,' they are communicating to Suzie that there is something wrong with her because she is mixed race—HYBRID."

"Ahhhh! Unfortunately, I get it now. I am slow at getting things now and then, but I get it now. Damnit, Damnit, Damnit!"

"Then, Mark, Suzie told me, 'Mommie, they follow hybrid with the word *fat*. It hurts me, Mommie. It hurts. I realize I am bi-racial and, like you, I am proud of it. But being called fat really, really hurts, and then they sometimes make pig noises. Others hear it and know what the *oinks* mean. It is because of what I look like. I do not even want to get out of bed in the morning sometimes.' Mark, hearing Suzie say that makes me sick to my stomach—I don't know what to do. What should we do, Mark, what should we do?"

"I don't know. I just don't know."

Suzie survived high school. The attempt to shame her into submitting to other people's perceptions of who she was, what she should look like, and who she wanted to be did not work. It did not crush her belief in herself. She continued to lack confidence in her self-image, and because of the body-shaming cruelty, she did not fully recover.

Ana and I supported Suzie as much as we could through her difficult teenage years. We repeated to Suzie over and over, "Suzie, just be yourself. We love you the way you are. You are a beautiful person in all aspects just the way you are—Suzie Blenchard—that is who you are. We love you so much."

In her senior year, Suzie added purple streaks to her hair. Megan Karla Brezos, had colored her hair too, MK's a bright red. When we thought it would be okay to ask, we ventured, "Honey, why did you color your hair?"

"Mommie and Daddy, I wanted to be my own person. Purple is my favorite color, so I added purple to my hair. I felt that doing so helped me to become someone in my own right. Therefore, I wasn't fat—I wasn't what people labeled me, 'a messed-up, mixed-race kid'—I was purple. I was just me. And, now that I am about to graduate, I am Suzie Blenchard and I am proud of it. I love you, Mommie and Daddy, and thank you for loving me while I grew to understand who I am."

After Suzie graduated from high school, she decided in college to major in history and education. She aspired to become a teacher. Her college essay communicated why.

Dear Admission's Committee:

I realize that some students are coached to write essays that will help them get into the college of their choice. I have neither been coached in writing this essay, nor has anyone read my reasons for applying.

My parents are both teachers. I did not show them this letter until I was ready to send it. After I showed this to them, I did not make any changes.

Once I am admitted to a college (hopefully yours), I will give this essay to my mother and father. It is the best gift I can think of giving them for all they have done for me, my brother, and their students.

I have seen my parents wrestle with issues they have encountered as teachers. I do not know how they do it, but they seem to love each of their students.

I do not want to imitate my parents because they are who they are, and I am who I am. However, I want to do what they do—teach. I realize how difficult teaching is and that is in part why I want to do it.

For my entire life, my parents have been teachers. I cannot think of anything else I could do that would be so satisfying and rewarding as becoming a teacher.

As I wrote above, I did not show this essay to my parents until I was ready to send this personal statement to you. When my parents read this college essay, they had tears in their eyes.

Upon gaining admission to the education department, I will be on my way to becoming a teacher. I will not be the same kind of teacher my parents have been and continue to be, but I will be a teacher nonetheless—my own kind of teacher. I will be myself and encourage my students to work toward achieving their hopes and dreams.

I want to someday help my students as much as my parents and my teachers have helped me.

Sincerely, Suzie Blenchard

Chapter 29: "Home"

From the day Claudia Pace took over Ken Lewiston's classroom in February, 1985, she taught students in Bailey High important subject matter and the critical thinking skills necessary for her students to be active citizens in the United States, and in the world.

"Mark, I love teaching here. Being with you and the rest of the faculty has helped to ground me. Now, I am grounded enough that I am going back. I am going home."

"I am not sure what you are talking about, Claudia," I admitted. "Going home? You don't mean like 'going home' in the religious sense, do you?"

"No. No, Mark. I mean going home in the place sense—where I belong. I know where I want to be at this stage of my life,"she explained.

"Where is that?"

"Well, you never forget your first teaching job," Claudia said. "I am returning to Appalachia. At the end of this school year, I am going back to work with those energetic young people, their loving parents, and the conscientious teachers I worked with in the hills and the hollows. The parents in those communities want a good education for their children. The teachers work hard to provide it, and the students can learn anything they want to when given a chance.

"Some of my former students are probably parents now carrying on the traditions of families in Appalachia—love for family, hard work, perseverance in the face of difficulty, a feeling of belonging, and a love of place. I have profound respect and admiration for the people I worked with. If they want me to, I am going to do whatever I can to help them. That is what I am determined to do."

"I know you well enough, Claudia, to know that when you are set on doing something, you follow through," I said. "But how about the trouble you were in and the fear it engendered when you were there?"

"Well, over a decade has passed, and times have changed. I have changed. I am not afraid anymore," she explained.

"As I said, you don't usually say something you intend to do and then not do it. When did you make the decision?" I asked. "I think I understand why, but when did you decide?"

"Oh, I have been thinking about going back for quite a while now. I realize I was there for just a short time, but the mountain air, the families struggling to make it, and the kids who want so much to learn make it the place I want to go back to and call home."

"You have mentioned in the past that you were afraid, but you said the fear is gone."

"Mark, I now realize fear can kill you," she went on. "Fear kills before you die. The fear of what might happen to me personally almost finished me. I was worrying about myself. Once you realize you are afraid, and you just panic, then you must find ways to overcome the fear or you die—even while you are alive—you die. You die because you are fearful all the time. I am no longer afraid."

"I can understand what you are saying, Claudia. I did not stand up for Ken Lewiston when I should have. I was afraid. I am trying to be courageous enough to confront my own fears."

"For my part in facing up, Mark, I am going to go back and try to teach in the school I left," Claudia declared. "I am also going to try to find Jeff, the assistant principal who protected me but was not careful enough for himself. I don't know where he is or even if I can find him, but I am going to try to follow his tracks. I hope he is still an educator because he was a good one. I also want to thank him for helping to protect me, so I could teach while I was there.

"Even though I am not originally from Appalachia, for some guttural reason, I consider it home. I have learned while teaching here at Bailey High and working with you all that I should trust my gut. I am trusting it now."

"We would hate to lose you, Claudia, but I—and I am sure your colleagues too—will support your decision to go back to what you consider home. The Bailey High students will be heartbroken, but I believe they will understand."

"Yes, I believe my current students will understand, and I hope so will the parents and students I am going back to," she said. "I am quite sure many of them are still in the community. If I can't get a teaching job immediately, I have saved enough money to live for a while.

"I will volunteer to help the community in any way I can. Besides, maybe some of my students from Bailey High will become teachers and come join me in teaching. I hope some of them will anyway."

Claudia resigned her teaching position in the Gorham, Massachusetts school system effective at the end of the school year in June, 1999.

As she left the building on her last day as a teacher at Bailey T. S. Memorial High School, Claudia said to me, "In addition to trying to meet with Jeff, the assistant principal who tried to help me in the mountain community, I want to find Clara. She was the student who had been urged to say that Jeff touched her. The accusation, though false, led to Jeff losing his job. If I can find them, I want to help Clara and Jeff in any way I can."

Chapter 30: "Heart"

"What does it mean to have 'heart?' We hear it all the time, but what does it mean to you, Mark?" John Browne asked.

"Over the time I have worked with you, John, and gotten to know you, I have learned a lot from you," I said. "You have introduced me to words and concepts like kleptocracy. Until you used the term, I had never heard the word or the concept. Now, maybe I have one for you. In Finland, the Finns have a word for our word, 'heart'—going beyond courage or 'sisu.'"

"Mark, you have me on this one—'beyond courage.' I get those words. But what does sisu mean when you say it goes beyond courage?"

"The term, sisu, is a concept that moves above, beyond, and through courage. There is no direct English equivalent. The closest I can come up with in our vernacular is the notion of HEART.

"I coached basketball for a while, and played sports. Having heart is that quality of pushing through despite the odds or the barriers. The team struggles through adversity. It doesn't give up—ever.

"It is like Karla Betts and how she lives her life. She does not waver. She just sets off—one foot in front of the other. She teaches resolutely, doggedly, and stays with a student until the student becomes a self-directed learner.

"Karla just flat out wills it! She combines her will and tenacious spirit with judicious obstinance. The sense she gives to her students is, 'I, as your teacher, will not let you fail. I care about you all and will be your cushion. I will not push or shove you, but I will challenge you and catch you when you fall.' Through her work as an educator, Karla illustrates determination to help learners achieve."

"Keep going, Mark."

"From watching Karla, Ken Lewiston, and other great teachers, I have observed that they are dedicated to doing the right thing in helping their students learn. That is what I think heart is. Within the parameters of the systems they work in, teachers figure out ways to help students learn.

"John, I faltered when it came to celebrating Ken Lewiston's life as a person and as a teacher. Educators like Ken and Karla don't falter. They know where they are going and go there.

"John Browne, I believe you have heart."

"I hope you are right, Mark," he said. "I mean—that I have it."

"John, I believe you do. For myself, though, I am still working on it."

Mr. M's Notebook: A Teacher's Life continues in Book Three. Book 3 is subtitled, "Memorial High." The tentative publication date for Book 3 is in 2021.

JOHN SPLAINE *has taught for over fifty years at the high school and college level. He taught in high schools in Maryland and New Hampshire, and taught in colleges in Colorado, Maryland, New Hampshire, and West Virginia. Splaine has written nonfiction books in government, history, and media literacy.*

www.ingramcontent.com/pod-product-compliance
Lightning Source LLC
Chambersburg PA
CBHW050409260626
47156CB00003B/933